In memory of
Nathan Freeman, M.D.,
Teacher and Friend,
and to Keir and Suzzy Dullea

LISA AND DAVID TODAY

OTHER BOOKS BY THEODORE ISAAC RUBIN, M.D.,
PUBLISHED BY MACMILLAN

Jordi
Lisa and David
The Winner's Notebook
The Angry Book
Compassion and Self-Hate

THEODORE ISAAC RUBIN, M.D.

Lisa and David Today

Their Healing Journey

from Childhood and Pain into

Love and Life

MACMILLAN PUBLISHING COMPANY   **NEW YORK**

COLLIER MACMILLAN PUBLISHERS   **LONDON**

Macmillan Publishing Company
866 Third Avenue, New York, N.Y. 10022
Collier Macmillan Canada, Inc.

Library of Congress Cataloging-in-Publication Data
√ *Rubin, Theodore Isaac.*
Lisa and David today.
Sequel to: Lisa and David.
I. Rubin, Theodore Isaac. Lisa and David.
II. Title.
PS3568.U293L57   1986   813'.54   85-23766
ISBN 0-02-605860-X

10 9 8 7 6 5 4 3 2 1

Designed by Jack Meserole

Printed in the United States of America

PREFACE

I have received many inquiries about Lisa and David since the publication of the book and the opening of the movie more than twenty years ago.

I didn't know what had become of them because the book I wrote so long ago was fiction, although I thought about them often enough during the years. What would have happened to them? What were the possibilities? Where are they now? The same questions many people asked me. Some people refused to believe they were fictional, and several psychiatrists asked me for clinical notes, which did not exist. But Lisa and David were fictional characters, and my stubborn head refused to give me a clue.

And then, more than twenty years after the opening of the film, I received a phone call from Keir Dullea, who so brilliantly played David in the film.

We got together, and Keir and his wife, Suzzy, suggested we do a screenplay—what happens twenty years later. Of course I said yes; we'd give it a try. And we tried. But the answers, despite many meetings and considerable struggle, refused to reveal themselves.

And then one morning—like an attack—it happened for me. I began to know what happened to Lisa and David. But I also knew that I had to use the old process, to write a book in order to get it all out. And then out it poured as if it had been sitting there all along these twenty-odd years.

This, then, is my twenty-fifth book, and I can think of no other I would rather have written or have published to occupy this position.

THEODORE ISAAC RUBIN

I

This is a love story of two exceptional children.

The place is a residential treatment center.

The time, one year after admission, is a crucial period in their lives during which communication becomes possible.

September 15, 1959—
September 15, 1960

ABIG fat sow, a big black cow—and how and how and how.

"A big fat cow, a big black sow—and how and how and how.

"A cow, a cow; a sow, a sow—big and fat, big and fat; so they sat—so they sat, they sat; so they sat."

She hopped around the room, first on one foot, then on the other. On her left foot she always said, "sow," and on her right foot, "cow." She sat down on the floor each time she said, "They sat, they sat." But in seconds she was up again—hopping around the room and, in a loud, clear, high-pitched voice, saying, "A cow, a cow; a sow, a sow—black, black, black, black, black, black, black, black." Her voice changed. She was shrieking now. Then she sat down, held her head with her hands, and moved it up and back, moaning softly. "Dark, dark, dark, dark, dark—so, so, so, so dark."

*

"Fuddy-dud-dud, fuddy-dud-dud-duddy—fud-fud-duddy fud-fud.

"Scudy-rud—rud-scud, rud-scud; duddy-scud fud rud, duddy scud fud rud."

She sat in the corner and repeated the sequence over and over again. John tried to engage her in a sensible

3

conversation—but to no avail. She listened to him, looked at him, and repeated the sequence again and again.

David listened and wondered what she meant. He finally gave up and thought about a big calendar clock he had seen a year ago.

That night before he fell asleep he had a fantasy. The sky was absolutely clear of clouds, the air cool, crisp, and dry. Thousands upon thousands of stars were visible. Planets could be seen, and the sun and moon, too. Beyond it all there were other suns and planets, other universes. They all moved perfectly, precisely, in exact relation to one another. The universes and galaxies and universes beyond them had all become part of a huge mechanism. It was the Universal Time Clock, and it measured Universal Time. He lay back and smiled, for after all he, David Green, was the Universal Timekeeper—or, better yet, Keeper of *the* Time—all Time.

He made sure the cover was tucked about him perfectly. He lay still—and fell asleep, his right hand clutched around the ancient teddy bear ear under his pillow. The light remained on all night.

*

"John, John, begone, begone—enough, enough of this stuffy stuff."

"Are you angry with me, Lisa?"

"Angry, angry—bangry, wangry—be gone, John; John, be gone."

"I guess you are angry. What is it that makes you so angry?"

4

"You foo, you foo—it's you, it's you—it's you, you foo; foo you, foo you."

She suddenly broke into a wild screaming laugh. She screamed and laughed continuously, imperceptibly inhaling air to laugh some more. After five minutes he interrupted her. "You're still angry, aren't you, Lisa?"

She stopped abruptly.

"You louse, louse—John is a louse, a big fat louse on a little gray mouse."

She looked up at the big man and grinned—an inane, foolish kind of grin. Her mood changed suddenly. The expression on her face became one of utmost seriousness. She suddenly charged away from the man and ran to the other side of the large reception room. She faced the wall and talked to herself in a barely audible whisper.

"He won't give me anything. He's big and fat and mean and why won't he give Lisa the crayons? He would give them to Muriel. He likes the Muriel me—but today I'm Lisa me, Lisa me."

Then she broke into a hop-skip-and-a-jump, quickly running around the walls of the room.

"Lisa, Lisa, is my name—today I'm the same—the same—the same, the same."

"May I speak to you, John?"

John turned to the tall, thin, teenage boy. David wore horn-rimmed glasses, was fastidiously dressed in a gray tweed suit, and conveyed the impression of utmost seriousness and dedication to intellectual pursuit. His pinched, thin, white face seemed too small for his long body. He spoke with the utmost precision.

"Why, yes, David. What would you like to say?"

5

"Thank you for your indulgence. Of late it has become increasingly difficult to find ears for my words. I've been studying your patient, or, since you are not a physician, shall I say student. I have come to several conclusions, which I feel time and further study by your staff will validate. Lisa is schizophrenic and is a child—I would say approximately twelve years of age. Therefore, my diagnosis would be childhood schizophrenia, undoubtedly of the chronic variety. However, diagnostic work is no challenge to me. I prefer to study the dynamic aspect of a particular case. Do you follow me?"

"Yes. Yes, indeed I do." John shook his head affirmatively.

"Good. Then I will continue."

Lisa was still hopping and skipping around the room, now periodically emitting a loud war whoop.

David chose his words carefully, the effort graphically demonstrated by his eyes and mouth. "Lisa has a most difficult time with authority or authoritarian figures. It is therefore extremely important that you adopt an attitude of complete permissiveness in your relationship with her. You must realize that this child has utmost difficulty with her emotions. Now, it is my belief that this difficulty is related to her obsession with speaking in rhymes. The rhyming serves as a decoy or camouflage for what she actually feels. I therefore think that you should not have refused her the crayons, even though she marked the wall."

Lisa stopped skipping and walked over to them.

"John, John, don't be gone—don't be gone."

"I'll see you later, David." He patted David on the shoulder.

6

The boy lurched away and screamed, "You touched me, you boor, you unmitigated fool—you touched me! Do you want to kill me? A touch can kill—you bastard, you rotten bastard!" His face was contorted with rage. He turned and left them, muttering to himself, "The touch that kills, the touch that kills," and carefully examining his shoulder.

*

"Can we sit down and talk a while?"

"Dr. White, I submitted to extensive testing, interviewing, and other such nonsense when I first came here, a year ago. I also spoke to you on occasion after that. Somehow I thought I'd go along with the routine here. New place—all right, I'd go along with the indignities. But there's a limit, even to cooperation—and, frankly, I don't care for more interviewing."

"You felt, New place, get off to a new start."

"Well, I suppose you could say that."

"David, it's not more interviewing I'm interested in. It's talking things over so that perhaps I can help you. After all, that's what we're both here for."

"You call me David—but I call you Dr. White."

"You don't have to."

"What do you mean?"

"You can call me Alan."

"All right, Alan." He smiled. "Let me think about it. When I'm ready, we'll talk."

"Suits me—You know where to find me; I'll be available."

"Suits me too." He walked out of the day room to the library.

She walked to where he was standing and placed herself directly in front of him. She looked up into his eyes and didn't budge. He stared back at her. In a completely serious voice she said, "Hello, hello, kiddo, kiddo."

He smiled. "Kiddo, hello; hello, kiddo."

She felt encouraged—and smiled ever so slightly at him.

"Me, the name; Lisa, the same."

For a minute he was puzzled, but when she repeated, "Me, the name; Lisa, the same," he realized she was asking him a question and then he caught on and answered.

"Me, the same; David, the name."

This time she smiled fully, and it wasn't a silly smile.

*

She passed David working at his table. On it was a large drawing of a clock.

Then she skipped about the room, chanting in a loud voice.

"Dockety dock, clock, clock; dockety dockety, clock clock clock.

"Hockety clock, dockety hock. Hock, hock; dock, dock."

Then she skipped over to John, who was sitting at the other end of the room. First she just stood in front of him. After a few minutes she slowly rocked from foot to foot. Five minutes later she rocked and chanted, this time in a low voice that only John could hear.

"Rockety rock, clock clock—dickety—rickety—lock lock."

John started to say something, but she ran off on a tour around the room.

*

He spent days poring over books. There were physics books, math texts, engineering manuals, and books on horology. When he wasn't reading, he spent hours at a drawing board making elaborate plans of watch and clock mechanisms.

Alan made several attempts to discuss his work with him, but David remained seclusive. At times he ignored Alan. At other times he said, "You're not really interested," or, "You wouldn't understand."

Then one day he picked up the plans he had drawn and locked them in his footlocker. From that time, he began to make more frequent visits to the day room.

*

"Do you have a watch?"

"Yes." He held out his wrist.

"Don't touch me." There was panic in his voice. "Please, don't touch me."

The man let his hand drop back to his side.

"Oh, you can hold your hand up. I'd love to see your watch—but let's not touch." He laughed a small, apprehensive laugh.

The man held his hand up again. David looked at the watch but made sure not to touch the man.

"That's not a very interesting timepiece. Is it the only one you own?"

"I have another, but right now it's not working."

"Oh? What kind is *it?*"

"A small, automatic, waterproof watch. I don't recall the make."

"I see. Probably not very good either. Do you know what kind of eccentric it uses?"

"Eccentric?"

"Yes—the rotor, the winding gear."

"I really don't know."

"Probably on a one-hundred-and-eighty-degree track. The better watches rotate fully, three hundred and sixty degrees."

"I see."

"Do you?" He stared at the man's eyes. "I don't think you do. So few people do. But I'll tell you anyway. There are automatic systems that work by bearings rather than rotor."

"How interesting."

David looked at him skeptically and said, "Perhaps we'll see each other again later; I have to spend a little time observing Lisa now."

"Could I possibly detain you for just a few minutes?"

"Detain me?" He rather liked the expression. "Yes, I suppose I could allow myself to be detained for several minutes."

"Tell me, are you interested in clocks, too?"

"Of course, I'm interested in watches, clocks, sundials—timepieces of all kinds. As a matter of fact, I had my clock execution dream last night."

"Clock execution dream?"

"I thought you would be interested. Frankly, I think you people put too much stress on dreams."

"Oh? Would you tell it to me anyway?"

"Yes, why not? This is a repetitive dream; I've had it time and again. It is always identical; only the characters are different."

"I see."

"No, you don't, but after I tell you, you will see.

"There's a big clock on a spike set in a large white bathtub. The tub is ten times larger than an ordinary one. The hands are huge, exquisitely sharp blades. I sit on a plush perch on the large hand. The face is white enamel. The numerals are sparkling diamonds. The movement is made by Patek Philippe. There are holes throughout the face to accommodate the heads of people sitting on little elevated stools on the other side of the clock. At ten o'clock the execution begins. The large hand, minute by minute, cuts through each neck, cutting off heads. The blood and heads fall into the bathtub."

"Who are the people?"

"They vary. Last night it was John." He pointed to the big man. "It was John—over and over again John —eight times. Who knows? Tonight maybe it will be you."

He walked away whistling.

*

"Did you analyze my dream—or does it require further study?"

"Neither."

"Neither?" He was interested now. "Meaning what?"

"A dream has meaning only in terms of the dreamer's symbols."

"Sounds like double-talk. Did you at least discern that I was crazy?"

"Crazy?"

"Yes, crazy, or—if you prefer—psychotic—though there's something vulgar about the word 'psychotic.' I prefer 'crazy'—more direct and at the same time homey.

"But what about my dream? You must have thought about it. Or will you evade my question with either more double-talk or psychiatric gibberish?"

"You sound angry in your dream—cutting off heads that way. Specifically, you sound angry at John—at least in the last dream you told me. And you sound angry now too."

He laughed a high-pitched, forced laugh full of mockery. "Brilliant, a brilliant analysis. Killing—hostility—John, anger at John. But how about the fiendish execution machine—the clock death dealer—the bathtub of heads and blood? Surely, surely, you detect the bizarre formulations of paranoid ideation, the intricate workings of a schizophrenic mind."

"Labels never interested me particularly."

"Well, what *does* interest you?"

"People, and what makes them tick."

"People ticking. I like that. Perhaps you *can* understand. I'll tell you an aspect of my clock dream that you did not think of." He waited patiently.

"The second-by-second, minute-by-minute cutting off of heads happens to all of us all of the time. The clock blades represent time, and the victims are all of us; and time slowly, slowly cuts us down—and there is no stopping it—no slowing it. On and on it goes, most accurately and effectively concentrating on batch after batch of victims from the second they are born. There is no escape."

They were silent.

*

"You said nothing when I interpreted my dream to you yesterday."

"That's right, I said nothing."

"Are you trying to get me angry?"

"No. I will not attempt to manipulate you in any way."

"Thanks," he said acidly.

After a few moments of silence he looked up. "Well, how come you said nothing?"

"Well, what do you think about it?"

"If you have to stay on good terms with me, don't touch me; don't touch me, and don't get Talmudic with me."

"I haven't touched you."

"That's true—but no Talmud, please."

"Stop being cute."

"You know what I mean. The business of answering a question with another question, this psychiatric, 'Well, what do you think about it?' So how come you *did* say nothing?"

"I wanted to give it some thought."

"Did you?"

"Yes, I did."

Now he spoke in a soft, childlike voice. There even seemed to be a slight tremor in his voice. "Alan, will you tell me *anything*?"

"All right, I will." He chose his words carefully, speaking very slowly. "I think you're afraid of death—terribly afraid."

"Of course, I am. Who isn't?"

"Now *you're* getting Talmudic."

David laughed a full, hearty laugh. Then he spoke. "I know that you know I'm afraid of death. You knew from the start how I can't stand to be touched—but the dream—I'm talking about the dream."

"So am I."

"Oh?" His eyebrow went up.

"Yes, it shows up in two ways. First, you're sitting on the blade killing your enemies—which will make you feel safer. And, secondly, *you're* sitting on the blade—controlling death and life."

"Enough, enough! I've had enough now. I'll see you later." He walked away.

*

"Sitting here talking to you reminds me of the first time they brought me to a psychiatrist."

"Oh?"

"Yes. You know—my first consultation." He laughed bitterly. "I was ten years old."

"What about it? How did it go?"

"When we got to the house, a big brownstone—just as we got there—a young girl, about eighteen, ran down the stairs—and into the street. A second later a very old, bent woman came running after her yelling, 'Come back.' But the young girl was way out of her reach. The old lady yelled, and I remember the exact

words—'If you don't come back for your shock treat-
ments, they will put you away.' She yelled back, 'Grandma,
I'm afraid. I can't. When I'm ready—not now—not now,
please.' "

"How'd you feel?"

He ignored the question and went on with the story.
"She didn't come back. A little crowd gathered, and they
all watched. In no time at all the girl was a block away.
The old woman kept chasing her but couldn't possibly
catch up. Everybody looked—but nobody helped; they
just stood and watched. You know what I think?"

"What?"

"I think everybody wanted to see that girl get away.
They were hoping she'd escape."

"Did you?"

"Yes."

"Then what happened?"

"I went in but hardly spoke to the psychiatrist at all.
You know what he said?"

"What?"

"That I'd be all right—nothing serious—for them
not to worry. An idiot—an M.D. idiot!"

"Are you angry with me, David?"

"What do you mean?"

"Would you like to call me an idiot? Would you like
to run from here? You know—like the girl?"

"That's a crazy idea."

"Is it?"

"Well, this place isn't the most fascinating, you know.
Anyway, I have to go to the library now."

He got up and left the room.

*

"Muriel, Muriel is a cigar—just like a car—a car, a car."

She skipped around the room quickly and now changed the rhythm slightly.

"Muriel, Muriel, is a cigar—and it smokes like a car, smokes like a car."

Then she changed to a hop-skip-and-a-jump and changed her rhyme again.

"Hop, skip, jump—Hop, skip, jump. I'm not a lump, I'm not a lump."

John stepped in front of her. She stopped short.

"No, you're not a lump. You're a girl, Lisa."

She walked around him and resumed skipping.

"I'm not a lump, and I like to jump. Lisa, Lisa is my name—but Muriel, Muriel is the same, the same."

*

"It's not the time or keeping time that interests me. It is the timepiece itself. The accuracy with which a particular instrument keeps time is directly proportional to the effort and skill of the creator."

"Creator?"

"Yes, creator!"

"Peculiar word to use in connection with a machine."

"I know. You would say 'artisan'—or, worse yet, 'technician'—or even 'mechanic' or 'manufacturer.' "

"Yes, I would."

"Yes, indeed. That is because to you a watch is only a machine used to serve a purpose—to tell time."

"And to you? What is it to you?"

He grinned slyly. "Thank you for asking me. I needed your question as an introduction. The timepiece to me, if it is a master timepiece, is a creation—a creation symbolizing the utmost skill and artistry. Think of the effort and skill involved in creating a clock that is nearly absolutely accurate. Think of the combination of these utterly precise instruments—and I call the clock parts 'instruments'—arranged in an almost perfect pattern for the purpose of harnessing time."

"Harnessing?"

He laughed an almost natural laugh. " 'Harness' is only a figure of speech—a slip." He became serious again. "I should say to measure time. You know—as one measures length, width, and breadth with a micrometer. To measure this, the most important dimension of all, the most dynamic—this ever-moving, ever-changing, and not changing at all—this most terrifying dimension of all—Time." He stopped and then a minute later, almost as an afterthought to himself, said, "If only we *could* harness time."

"We can."

"We can?" He looked up at Alan, his face a picture of alert curiosity.

"Perhaps we cannot change the time allotted to us—perhaps we cannot add even one extra second to it. But if we use time in our behalf, if in the time of our lives we have freedom of choice—so that we have grown even one iota, in one split second in all the time of times—then we *have* harnessed this dimension."

"That is a difficult thought to digest. I must give it some thought."

"And time?" Alan smiled.

"And time," David repeated. He turned and walked away.

*

She stopped in front of David, stared at him, then said, "David, David looks at me—but what does he see, what does he see?"

He looked up from the desk. "It's Lisa, Lisa whom I see—staring at me, staring at me."

She smiled at him and came a little closer. He stood up quickly and walked a little distance away. "Don't touch, don't touch—me don't touch. All else will do—but please no such."

She stood still and remained smiling.

"Touch, such—such touch—foolish talking, foolish squawking."

He repeated, "Yes, but—no such, no touch."

She agreed. "No such, no touch."

*

"You made a friend?"

"Friend? What are you talking about?"

"Lisa. I noticed you talking to her."

"Oh, that. Well, don't get any ideas. My social adjustment or any other psychiatric descriptive nonsense you want to apply just doesn't apply here."

Alan smiled.

"What's so funny?"

"Funny? Oh, nothing funny. I was just thinking that I take great pains not to use so-called psychological technical language, and yet here you accuse me of doing just that anyway."

18

"All right, that's true," he said grudgingly. "You talk straight enough; it was the others. Does that make you feel better?"

"Yes, it does," Alan said seriously. "It does make me feel better."

"Good for you." David smiled. "Can I get back to this Lisa-child business now?"

"Yes, please do."

"Thank you," he said, clenching his jaw. "Thank you, very much."

Alan remained quiet.

"As I was saying, Lisa is not a friend. I have no friends. If I did have a friend—which is rather inconceivable—it is unlikely that I would choose a twelve- or a thirteen- or fourteen-year-old infant—obviously my intellectual inferior. I talk to Lisa only because she interests me clinically. I would hardly bother to do something arduous and boring as to talk in rhymes for the mere purpose of a ridiculous friendship."

"I see."

"Good."

He walked to the other side of the large day room to wait for Lisa to come down from her own room.

Lisa walked into the day room. Her head was bent, and she walked slowly.

David approached her. He said nothing. John and Alan spoke quietly on the other side of the room.

"Lisa, Lisa, do you want to talk; or would you rather take a walk?"

"Talk, walk. Don't you see—today I'm sick; I'm not me." She walked away and he followed. Her mood seemed to change abruptly. She skipped around the room but said, "Today I'm low, low; so, David, go, go, go." He walked away.

Alan walked to him. "You look angry."

"Angry, bangry," he grinned. "No, I'm not angry. It's just that she's hard to reach."

"Maybe she just doesn't feel well just now."

"I have a feeling that she's trying to tell me that she's menstruating."

"Oh, maybe she is. How do you feel about it?"

"Feel! Is that all you think of—feel, feel? I don't feel. I don't feel a thing. Now what do you feel about that?"

"I feel you're angry. As Lisa would say, 'angry, bangry.' "

"I don't think it's funny, and I don't think you understand Lisa or me. I'm not angry—and I'll tell you what I feel—hungry. Yes, hungry. That's what I feel—hungry." He turned to leave the room.

"Well, feeling hungry is a feeling." But David paid no attention and walked out.

*

She printed on a white piece of paper with black crayon and then held it up to him. YOU RIME. TALK PLAIN—STRAYT.

"Oh, that makes it easier. It's not s-t-r-a-y-t; it's s-t-r-a-i-g-h-t—and r-h-y-m-e not r-i-m-e."

She printed STRAIGHT and RHYME.

"Can you spell out loud?"

NO, she printed in huge letters.

"All right, all right—nobody is going to force you, Lisa."

NOT LISA—WHO LISA——MURIEL—MURIEL
—I—ME—MURIEL.

"Lisa, Muriel. Frankly, I prefer the name Lisa."

She pointed at him with her index finger—and then came a little closer. He backed away, but she followed.

"Lisa, don't touch me. Now be careful, don't touch me!"

She returned to the table and printed MURIEL in huge letters, filling a whole piece of typing paper. She held it up to him.

"Yes—I see. All right, Muriel, Muriel, don't touch me!"

She smiled a little half-smile and returned to the table and sat down.

*

Lisa and John sat at the table, the paper and pencils before them, saying nothing.

Finally, after some twenty minutes, he asked if she would care to write something, or perhaps draw.

She shook her head no. She then walked to the screened window and looked out and watched the clouds. To her it seemed as though they were running after one another in slow motion. After a few minutes she returned to the table, picked up the pencil, and drew three clouds; then she drew them closer together—then overlapping, and finally one cloud within another. She then drew a big black X through them all.

David and Alan came into the room, busily talking in low voices.

Once again she picked up the pencil and printed, DAYVED.

John said, "Very good—very good, indeed."

She printed, DAYVED, again, this time in much larger letters.

John took another sheet of paper and printed, DAVID—DAVID GREEN. "This is another way of spelling his name—the way he spells it. Green, you know, is his second name."

She took a fresh sheet of paper and printed, DAVID GREEN——MURIEL.

She looked up at him and pursed her lips—but it wouldn't come. She couldn't think of her second name. Tears ran down her cheeks.

"Brent," he said. "Brent."

She tore the sheet up into little pieces; then took a fresh one and printed:

MURIEL LISA

and then broke into uncontrollable sobbing.

*

"Lisa, Lisa, why must we rhyme? It's so hard to do and takes so much time."

"Funny David, can't you see? Rhyming stops her, she then can't be."

He looked up with the surprise of discovery. "That's it, that's it. That's why you rhyme; you suppress Muriel by rhyming. You suppress her—now I see."

She darted away.

"Lisa, I'm sorry. I'll rhyme; yes I will rhyme—slime, climb, rhyme. Lisa, Lisa," he called. But she was away now, far away.

The panic overtook her. She ran around the room quickly.

"Climb, slime, climb, slime—I can't rhyme; oh, I can't rhyme." She began to cry. "I can't rhyme, I can't rhyme."

And a buzz in her head got louder. Then it grew and became a voice. The voice filled her head; it terrified her. And then she became calm. She sat down at the table with John.

"Do you feel better, Lisa?"

She looked up at him and laughed, a deep sarcastic laugh. There was no sound. But its expression was clear on her face.

"Won't you talk?"

Again she laughed the soundless laugh.

"I see, you won't talk." He handed her the sheet of paper.

She drew a huge cigar and colored it bright red. Underneath it she printed:

I AM MURIEL NOW.

*

"I had a peculiar dream last night."

"Oh? Would you care to tell me about it?"

"Yes, I will tell you. I searched and searched. It was terribly hard. But then I found it—the Lost Continent. It was a vast place and yet it was small. There were only thin, tall people there. They all wore glasses and were immaculately clean and young. Everybody knew that they must not touch each other. I felt that I'd found— well, as if I'd found home."

"You were comfortable there."

"Yes, I was comfortable there," he said softly.

"Everybody in the dream sounds like you—at least from the outward description."

23

"I suppose you could say that.

"Say, do you think it's because I would like to find a place—that is for me? You know, a place where all the others, the you's, would be strangers."

"That may be," Alan replied gently. "But as you said, the continent was a lost one. Perhaps, David, it would be easier to get to be able to live in this, the world that isn't lost."

"Perhaps, but I don't know." He shook his head as if to clear it. "I mean I'll have to think about it some more."

*

Lisa's heads poked through the holes. There was only one Lisa sitting on a high stool behind the clock. But she had eight faces, and each of them wore a different expression. One looked silly; another was frightened; the third had a crafty look; and the fourth laughed a high-pitched screaming kind of laugh. He couldn't make out the expressions on the other four but knew that they were all different. Then the sixth from the numeral twelve—and he thought, Twelve noon or twelve midnight—started to talk. "David, David, I'll talk to you, because that is what I like to do." The first face came into focus. It smiled warmly, even tenderly. He thought of his teddy bear—and its soft cloth ear.

Then ten o'clock rang out, and the hands started to move. But a funny thing happened. All the heads came into focus, and the faces looked sweet and gentle. And the hands stopped. He yelled, "Go on, go on!"

But they wouldn't budge. He pleaded. "Please, go on." But they didn't move. Then he screamed, "Oh, God, my God!"

His screaming woke him. He was drenched in sweat. He felt very stiff. This was followed by an unfamiliar funny feeling, and then he became very frightened. He quickly stuck his hand under the pillow and found the soft ear of the ancient teddy bear. He brushed his nose, then his eyelids, and then his lips with it. It made him feel better.

Before too long he forgot the nightmare and fell asleep.

*

He sat at the table reading the math book.

She slipped the note on the table and then stood still. He read it.

PLAY WIT ME.

He looked up at her.

With controlled anger he said, "How stupid can you be! It's 'with' not 'wit'—with, with, not wit. Now, go, leave me be."

She turned around and started to walk away—but suddenly turned again and approached him. But she had changed, looked different, and he got up, a little frightened, ready to leave the room.

"Leave me, be me. David, shmavid, shmavid David."

"Play, play another day," he said, trying to placate her.

But she continued bitterly, "David shmavid—shmavid David."

"All right!" He clenched his teeth. "Lisa, shmisa, shmisa, Lisa."

He turned and left the room.

*

"Finish squawking and talking. Finish talking and squawking. Skipping, jumping, jumping, skipping—that's what I want to do.

"David, skip and jump with me, and I'll skip and jump with you."

"I won't skip and I won't jump, but I'll walk while we talk."

"No squawk talk, no talk squawk—but let's walk, let's walk."

They walked around the day room and said nothing. They were careful not to touch each other.

*

A nurse told him that Lisa did not feel well and could not come down to the day room. David sat down in an easy chair in one of the small side rooms. After several minutes Alan walked in and sat a short distance from him.

"A penny for your thoughts."

"These are worth considerably less than that."

"I see."

They sat silently for some ten minutes.

"Do you know what I was thinking about when you came in?"

"No, what?"

"Well, just before I came here—that is, to this place—an odd incident occurred."

26

"Oh, what's that?"

"I had to go uptown to get a clock catalogue. Against my better judgment and with much trepidation, I took the train—the subway. As soon as I got on it, I knew it was a mistake. It looked filthy, but I had to get uptown—and at least it was almost empty. Well, we came to De Kalb Avenue, and a load of people walked in. I wanted to get out—but couldn't without bumping at least one of them—and then the train started, and it was too late. I stood in a corner of the car; I steeled myself but it was no use—I felt very sick. Then we came out of the tunnel, onto the bridge. Being on the bridge made me feel even more closed in—more—well, caught. I had violent palpitations, felt I couldn't breathe." He hesitated and then looked at Alan's eyes. "I guess I thought I'd have a heart attack."

Alan waited, but David didn't go on. He seemed to be daydreaming—away from the room.

"Then what happened?" Alan asked in a whisper.

"Oh, well, that's the funny part of the story—what happened next. And, you know, it all happened within minutes—from the beginning of the Manhattan Bridge to Canal Street."

Alan waited.

"It was one of the few times I thought of my mother and father. Suddenly they just occurred to me, and for a second or two I felt better. Then I pictured them yelling at each other, and I felt awful again. That's when the funny thing happened. I saw this woman—a heavy, smiling, Jewish Mamma kind of woman. She was with her three children. There was a boy eighteen, a boy thirteen, and a little boy about six. The little boy was leaning against the thirteen-year-old, sleeping and sucking his thumb. And they were all talking together. Mostly the conversation was about the little boy—how cute he was—Is he still sleeping? Let him sleep, let him sleep—that kind of talk. You know, she didn't have three children; she had four. I became the fourth. I was part of that family—one of her boys—and the funny thing is, the sickness left. I didn't even get off at Canal—I rode right on to Fifty-seventh. Funny, isn't it?" He laughed. "She never knew she had another boy."

"No. I don't think it's funny at all."

His face became serious again. "I'm going to take a walk in the yard now."

"Would you like me along?"

"As you wish."

They got up and left the room.

*

He sat with the large physics textbook in front of him. But he didn't look at the material. Periodically he glanced over the top and stared at John and Lisa. They sat at the low table, printing.

That bastard, he thought, that vicious bastard. He'd like to see me dead—I know—I just feel it. I'll watch. I'll watch—touch me, touch me. Probably says vicious things about me. She doesn't understand anyway—how could she—that silly child—that man—a fool, a complete fool—therapist—therapist and he touched me. How he hates me, how he hates—that coarse, stupid, dirty, ridiculous bastard. He doesn't understand that child. Look at the man—big, fat, stupid, vicious, insensitive. Probably wears an American watch—a Mickey Mouse

28

American watch. No accuracy in that man—no precision—clumsy, stupid clumsy. I hate to even look at him.

He got up and stalked out of the room with his physics book.

*

There was a large clock. It ticked steadily as the hands slowly moved around the face. He stood under the large hand and held it, trying to keep it from moving. But it was too strong and kept going. He hung from it—but it moved with him on it. He threw things at it—it kept moving. He struck it again and again with an ax—but it didn't make a dent. He hit it with the sledgehammer. There was a hollow ring that changed to a laugh. The laughing was like a ticking now, and the laughing-ticking said, "Can't stop me, me me me—can't stop me, me me me." He screamed in his sleep and woke up feeling mixed up. But he quickly got up and in so doing re-established his equilibrium.

He went to the bathroom and showered. He soaped himself scrupulously, accounting for every millimeter of skin surface. He soaped and showered eight times, the entire operation taking an hour and ten minutes. He shaved with utmost care, making absolutely certain that no hair remained on his face. After urinating and defecating, he washed his hands six times, brushed his teeth three times, and then carefully combed his hair, making sure that the part was perfectly straight. His entire bathroom activity took two hours, but he had plenty of time until breakfast. After he finished dressing, it was only seven-thirty.

*

She looked at herself in the mirror. The girl who looked back at her seemed indistinct, blurred. She tried to make her more real, but she still looked wispy, faded, as if she would disappear. Then she tried to make her more real by making silly faces. She blew her cheeks up with air. She stuck her tongue out. She smiled foolishly. Nothing worked; the image was still vague. Then she clenched her teeth and curled her lip; an angry face looked back at her—but it looked real, of substance, alive. But the anger in it scared her. She turned away from the mirror—and was out of the room, away from the hateful face.

For several days she didn't dare look at the mirror in her room.

She lay in bed and looked up at the ceiling. A little light came through the shaded window. She could just make out a vague shadow on the ceiling. She put her hand on her face. Then her hand seemed to be separated from the rest of her. It was as if it had a life of its own. She regarded it in a detached way—but at the same time concentrated on it so that it absorbed her completely.

It lightly touched her hair and mussed it up in an almost affectionate way. Then it traced the outlines of her nose and mouth almost as a blind person would. Then it came down to her neck and clenched it tightly. At the same time, she felt a kind of bubbling laughing in her head and got frightened. Then she grasped her right hand with her left and removed it from her neck.

It moved downward. It touched her small breasts and nipples, and this felt pleasant. Then it went over her belly to her thighs, to her clitoris. It rubbed her clitoris, and it felt nice. After a while fear and tension was almost gone, and she fell asleep. When she woke in the morning, her hand was part of the rest of her again.

*

He lay in bed, and at first he didn't sleep. Then he had a fantasy. After a while the fantasy slipped into a dream as he finally fell asleep. There was a great clock—a huge precision instrument made up of extremely complicated parts. It read four o'clock, and chimes rang out four o'clock. Then a voice—neither male nor female, a metallic voice—said, "It's four—one, two, three, four o'clock." Then the clock stopped. It would go no further. Then for an important reason he added twelve to the four, and it added up to sixteen. But the clock still didn't move. After a while the clock turned back to one again, and this time went to sixteen o'clock. But it stopped short at sixteen and would go no further. The clock then turned into the most complicated mechanism possible. It was an electronic, atomic clock. It was very strong. But it could not break through sixteen. He then had a funny sensation. Half of him felt different from the other half. It was as if an invisible line was drawn through the middle of him, dividing him into two hemispheres. He looked back at the clock. It was trying desperately to move past sixteen. It seemed to move past — a second and a half past—and then he stopped dreaming.

When he woke, he had a fleeting thought—he was

trying to charge through a concrete wall but made no impression on the smooth, hard surface.

He spoke to Alan later that day.

"Do you know anything about electronic clocks?"

"No—but sounds interesting."

"I'm sixteen today."

"Oh! Happy birthday."

"About that talk we had—"

"Which?"

"You know, some time ago. Controlling time."

"Oh, yes. What about it?"

"This business of choice. If you have a choice over the time, you said."

"What about it?"

A look of disgust came over his face. "Stop this pedantic what-about-it stuff! I'm asking you about it. It's your production, so can you spare a few words to elaborate on it?"

"Choice means just that—choice. When people are not well, much of what they do is done because they have to do it. But if they get better and become themselves, then they are free to do as they please; they have a choice."

"You mean compulsive versus noncompulsive."

"You could say that—though I prefer to use plain language rather than technical terms."

"Thanks for being so condescending. Also thanks for the 'they' routine—when you mean me." He suddenly got angry. "Me! That's right, me. Me—David. Real compulsive nut—aren't I?"

Alan started to answer, but David suddenly got up and walked away.

*

"David, David, here you are; come with me far, oh far." She looked up at him beseechingly.

"Not today, not today—tomorrow I say, tomorrow I say." He walked to Alan's office. The door was open.

"Hello, David. Please come in."

"She irritates me—certainly can be a nuisance."

"She?"

"That Lisa child."

"She annoys you?"

"Well, sometimes she—oh, I don't know. It's like—oh!" He threw his hands up in exasperation.

"Everybody is irritated at times."

"Is that supposed to make me feel better?"

"Better or worse—it's simply a statement of fact."

"Statement of fact—I like that. Well, I'll tell you a fact. I had a really crazy dream last night; a real . . ." He looked for the words but couldn't find them.

"A real lulu."

"Yes." He smiled. "Could say that—a real lulu. You want to hear it?"

"Sure do."

"I had a funny feeling in my stomach and then the feeling turned to a pain—a gnawing kind of pain. Then in my dream while I had the pain I had a fantasy at the same time. The fantasy involved my having a rat in my belly—which was slowly but methodically eating through my diaphragm trying to get to my heart. The next thing,

33

my fantasy changed: instead of a rat, there she was—that ridiculous Lisa child. And her face—that sweet, insipid smile of hers."

He waited. Alan said nothing.

"Aren't you going to say anything?"

"Do you want me to?"

"I don't care. But—if you want to—go ahead."

"I think Lisa is getting to you."

"Getting to me?"

"Yes, getting to your feelings. Perhaps you're beginning to like her."

"Like her! How ridiculous can you get!" He spoke between clenched teeth. "She's a clinical study—only clinical. Sometimes you sure can be ridiculous." He got up and left the room—muttering, "So ridiculous, so ridiculous; almost as stupid as that bastard John."

*

He ran faster and faster but knew that it was not fast enough. He had a pain in his side and was out of breath but kept running. The thought flashed through his mind that he should have been more of an athlete. But it was too late now. He kept running, and the pain in his side now extended itself to his chest. It became unbearable, but he had to keep going. He looked down. It was there all right, and he couldn't jump to the side. He could run, but some kind of magnetic pull kept him glued to the treadmill. But it wasn't a treadmill; it was a clock, a linear clock. It was a ribbon of ever-moving time that kept disappearing into a huge abyss of nothing. He ran counterclockwise, but time ran out a little faster—and every second brought him closer to the nothingness. Then he realized that running served no purpose; he could not escape the movement of time. And then he was in the nothingness—falling; falling through space —and there was a clock in his head that ticked off the seconds; time was running out, fast. He would soon become part of the nothingness. The ticking stopped— and he woke.

For several days he spoke to nobody. He went to meals and spent the rest of the time reading books and drawing plans of elaborate clocks. He did not return Alan's greeting.

Then one day, after nearly a week had passed, he returned to the day room. Alan walked up to him.

"Good to see you back, David."

"Good! You mean good for you. You like winning, don't you?"

"Winning?"

"You know what I mean. Winning—between us. Me being here again."

"I didn't know we were having a battle. As a matter of fact, I consider us both on the same side—your side."

"My side?"

"Yes, your side—to help you. After all, that's what I'm here for."

"Sounds corny."

"What does? That anybody should want to help you?"

"That's enough of this psychology. Let's talk of other things."

"Suits me."

"Alan, have you ever considered the possibility of a radio clock?"

"You mean a radio alarm?"

"No, no. That's just a gadget everybody has. I mean—well, this is a new idea. You wouldn't say anything; I mean, I want secrecy—absolute secrecy."

"Everything you tell me is confidential."

"Well, people would wear this clock receiver which would be timed in to a central electronic device—through which they would constantly be informed of the exact time."

"If they were interested."

"What do you mean?"

"Well, I think the idea shows much ingenuity—but few people are interested in constantly having the exact time."

He did not answer and just sat still.

After a few minutes Alan asked, "Have I offended you, David?"

"No."

"David, what made you so angry? You didn't talk to me for about a week."

"It was my feeling."

"Yes, what feeling?"

"I felt you and John were talking about me—that he said vicious things about me. Did—I mean, did he?"

"No."

"No?"

"No."

"The feeling was very strong."

"Your feeling about John must be very strong."

"I hate him! He's an uncouth, savage, ridiculous idiot. I don't see how he'll ever help that child."

"Lisa?"

"Yes, Lisa. What time is it?"

"Ten minutes to lunchtime." Alan smiled. "David,
how come you own no watch?"

"There isn't a timepiece made that interests me.
They're grossly inaccurate—clumsy junk. I don't like
them next to my skin. Some day, when I make one—a
real piece—a masterpiece—then I'll carry it. It won't be
a wristwatch anyway."

"Oh? Why not?"

"They can never be really accurate. Besides, I don't
like to constrict my wrist. I'm hungry."

"Good. Just about time for lunch."

"I've been thinking about this business of Lisa getting
to me."

"Yes."

"Well, she is a rather interesting child."

"Interesting?"

"Well, there are times she—well—when her face is
interesting-looking."

"She is nice-looking. Beautiful eyes."

"Nice, beautiful—I didn't say that."

"No, you didn't. I did."

"She does have expressive eyes."

"I think so."

"But she can be silly."

"Silly?"

"Well, this jumping about—rhyming and the rest."

"Perhaps she can't help herself?"

"Perhaps? There's no perhaps about it. You know very well she can't help herself. After all, she is a sick child."

"Yes, I agree."

*

FOURTEEN AND A HALF
FOURTEEN YEARS—AND SIX—MONTHS
"Very good—very good, indeed. That's how old you are now—well, to be exact, a week ago."

YOU—YOU, she printed.

"Me?" he said. "If you want to know how old I am, print the question and end with a question mark."

HOW OLD ARE YOU?

"I am sixteen and a half years old—sixteen years and six months."

JOHN, HOW OLD IS HE?

"Frankly, I don't know and I don't care. But I would judge about three—no, maybe only two."

ALAN—ALAN?

"I don't know—perhaps forty or forty-five or so."

A week later she spoke to John:

"You're three, three, three; you see, you see.

Maybe two, two.

Poor you, poor you."

*

"I notice you ignore all the other people here."

"Your observation is correct."

"Do you ever have any desire to socialize with any of them?"

38

"Socialize—that's quite a word to use for a place like this."

"How so?"

" 'Socialize' implies freedom of choice with whom you have social contact. You should know about the phrase 'freedom of choice,' since you are always using it."

"Always?"

"Almost. Not always—sometimes. Anyway, since talking with people must only be with people here—how much freedom can there be in such a social selection?"

"You can freely choose from the people here."

"Thanks, but no thanks. There's no freedom in that—and you know it. It's like—well, like asking about an opinion of Republican policy among an all-Democratic group. Besides which, there's another implication that I sense."

"What's that?"

"Well, it's that even though we here in this institution are all individuals and as such different, being here, having the same problems, ought to make us enough the same—that is, people think we ought to be enough the same—so as to give us the desire to socialize. Let me tell you I am not the same. None of us are. We may be here—but we're still different."

"I'm glad you recognize that everyone is different, because we all are different. As for problems, everybody has them—in and out of here. But sounds to me as though you're protesting too much—reacting too strongly."

"What do you mean?"

39

"Well, like being here does in fact make you the same as everyone else—and that talking to them will add to the similarity, and as such is dangerous."

"I don't know what you're talking about. Besides, I have some research to do now." He left for the library.

Three days later he returned another patient's greeting and later on beat him in a game of chess.

*

She sat in the corner of the room and said in a loud, clear voice,

"Holly, golly—golly, holly. Golly, holly—holly, golly."

When John approached her, she stopped talking. As soon as he left, she began and repeated over and over again,

"Holly, golly—golly, holly. Golly, holly—holly, golly."

A week later the room was stripped of Christmas decorations.

*

The snow lasted more than an hour. They searched all over and couldn't find her.

Then John discovered her hiding place. She was in his coat closet. She stood perfectly still inside the heavy tweed coat, using it as a tent. When she came out, the snow had stopped. She skipped and jumped around the room yelling, "Snow, snow, go, go. Go, go—snow, snow."

John spoke to her. "Were you afraid, Lisa? Were you afraid of the snow?"

But she paid no attention and continued to jump about the room.

40

"Go, go—snow, snow. Snow, snow—go, go."

Then it began again, and she ran for the closet. This time he put a little stool in the tent, and she sat on it until the snow stopped.

She went to the new poster on the wall and looked at it. It was from a travel agency and pictured a beautiful green farm scene with snow-capped mountains in the background. John came up beside her.

She turned to him and said, "So green, so nice—no snow, no ice."

"Yes, Lisa. Green and nice—no snow, no ice," he repeated back to her.

She went to the table near the window, sat down, and drew on a large white sheet of paper. John sat next to her and watched. When she finished, there was a fairly good replica of the poster in miniature. They took it to the wall and tacked it up next to its parent poster.

She stood back and looked—then said, "No snow, no ice—green and nice."

That night in bed she spoke to herself. "Green grass—tall, warm, green grass." She pictured herself putting her face into it. It was warm and tickled. After a while she fell asleep.

*

"A page to write my age—to write my age, I need a page." She skipped about the room slowly, repeating again and again, "A page, a page to write my age—to write my age, I need a page."

John stood in her path, and she stopped short. "Here,

Lisa. Here is a piece of paper and a pencil—a page to write your age."

She sat down at the table and printed,

I HAVE A PAGE TO WRITE MY AGE—I'M FOURTEEN AND A HALF THATS NO LAFF.

She looked up at him and smiled. It wasn't a silly smile.

David walked over to her and said nothing. She went to one of the tables and sat down. He sat opposite her. She printed on the pad,

LET US SIT AND TAUK.

"You mean let us sit and talk and write, and talk is spelled t-a-l-k."

YOU PLAY GAME BOY. She pointed to the other side of the room.

"Yes, I played a game of chess with the boy—with Robert."

Her face crackled into a silly grin. She got up and skipped away from him.

"Game, game—boy, poy—chess, chess; mess, mess."

She paid no more attention to him that day.

*

"Do people really change, Alan? Or I should say, can people change?"

"Yes, I believe they can, and I believe they do."

"I don't know. It's easy to say. You're so glib about it."

"It is easy to say, but that doesn't make it less true. People change; people grow!"

"Words, words—just words."

42

"No, not just words. People change. Look at Lisa."

"Lisa?"

"Yes, Lisa. She writes more, her speech makes more sense—she certainly has improved her relationships here."

"Relationships?"

"Well, like with you. She's friendlier."

"Big change," he grunted.

"Little changes can be important. Growth is a slow process. It doesn't happen suddenly—it's really hard work."

"Hard work, slow process. Funny, I just remembered something."

"Oh? What?"

"When I was very young—maybe seven or eight—two things happened the same day. Completely unimportant—but I never forgot them. About once every year or so I remember them."

"Yes. What were they?"

"If this is psychotherapy, I don't know how it helps —and yet . . ."

"Yet what?"

"Well, I do like to talk—when I'm in the mood. Alan, do you think—well—me here, I mean . . ."

"Yes, you're changing too, David. And I guess I am also."

"Well, anyway, what I remembered was this. My mother and I were on the train going from Brooklyn to Manhattan. We sat near the door. We were both afraid of not being able to get out on time when we'd get to our station."

"Did she say she was afraid?"

"No, but she was; I just knew it."

"I'm sorry for interrupting your story."

"That's OK." He smiled. "Anyway, on Atlantic Avenue a very old lady got on the train. She was very thin and dressed poorly, but she kept smiling all the time. As thin and poor as she was, she seemed happy. Anyway, I then noticed she had a package. She sat down next to a heavy, well-dressed woman and then opened the package. She took out three dolls. They were small but exquisite dolls; each feature was perfect, and they were very elaborately dressed. She fussed with each one—straightening the dress, fixing the hair—and all the time smiling and happy. The next thing, the woman next to her started a conversation with her, and in a few minutes I saw her hand the old lady some money and take one of the dolls—a dark one. Then the old lady moved to another seat next to another well-dressed woman and started fussing with the dolls again."

"Did she sell another one?"

"I don't know. We got to our station about then. Well, when we got out and walked a while—the second thing happened that I never forgot."

"What's that?"

"We came to this nice quiet street, and there was a woman cooing and kissing and patting and cuddling a baby in a carriage. When I got up close, I looked at the baby. It was deformed. I don't remember now—but it was abnormal; even its face wasn't right. But she didn't seem to know about it. She just went on kissing and loving that baby. I thought about it a lot that night. Couldn't sleep—that and other nights."

"Where were you going with your mother that day?"

44

"I don't remember—but it was probably to the doctor."

"The doctor?"

"Yes. Around that time they kept taking me to the doctors. I was too tall, too thin, underdeveloped—all kinds of faults." He looked into Alan's eyes. "You know something?"

"Yes?"

"They really were stupid. There's Lisa. I'll see you later."

*

"You know, I haven't had a clock dream in about a month."

"In a month, you say?"

"That's right—at least that."

"I noticed you playing chess."

"Yes, I've been playing with Robert Salkin. Not a bad player—but not much competition. I always win."

"Oh."

"You know something I observed?"

"What's that?"

"I think Lisa gets irritated when I play with Robert." He shrugged his shoulders. "Part of her sickness, I guess."

*

"David, David, look at me—who do you see, who do you see?" She looked up at him questioningly.

He observed her in a clinical, detached way, as he would a clock or a watch, but said nothing.

"David, David—say to me; say to me what you see."

45

After she repeated the rhyme some ten times, he finally answered. "A girl, a girl—I see a girl. Who looks like a pearl—a small black pearl."

"A girl, a girl—a small black pearl. Girl, pearl; pearl, girl.

"Pearl, girl; girl, pearl. I'm a girl, a pearl—a black girl pearl."

She ran to the other side of the room.

"John, John—I'm a girl, a girl—a pearl of a girl."

David sat by himself at the table thinking of rhymes. It was more difficult than he had anticipated, and such silly things came up: Come away with me—just you and me—away, far away, to a distant sea.

Then he changed it: Come away with me to a distant sea, a distant sea.

Then he thought, slime, slime—climb, chime, dime dime—girl, pearl, pearl girl. A distant land—foreign sand—no touching with a filthy hand. Lisa, Lisa, name the same—enough, enough of this stuffy stuff—stuffy stuff.

He smiled to himself. Enough of this stuffy stuff, indeed—enough of this nonsense.

He got up and went to the library. For a while he sat and did nothing. Then for over two hours he drew an elaborate plan of a clock. It was a precision instrument capable of nearly absolute accuracy. But it didn't satisfy him. He turned it over and drew the face. When he finished the numerals, he recognized the execution machine. He quickly tore it up and threw it into the wastebasket.

46

*

She lay in bed and thought about the snow. It seemed so gray and strange and cold. She pictured the sky opening up and tons of it falling down all at once. She pulled the cover over her head, shutting out the little light that came through the shaded window. She remembered the smell of John's coat. Remembering the tweediness of it almost made her sneeze. After a while thoughts of the snow disappeared, and she felt better. After much tossing and turning—so that the bed looked like the scene of a great upheaval—she fell asleep, curled up at the foot of it, the cover over her head.

The dream was one of the few clear ones she ever had. There was a great snowstorm and she had to get to the other side of the huge square. She couldn't move. Then she saw John's coat—it was very long and stretched clean across the square. She still couldn't move. Then she saw David on the other side—beckoning to her—and she heard his voice calling, "Lisa, Lisa, Lisa, Lisa—" She stepped on the coat.

When she woke in the morning and looked out the window, she saw the sun, bright and warm.

It was a lovely spring day.

John and Lisa sat together at the large round table in his office. She looked through the magazine, slowly turning the pages and studying the pictures. John read the newspaper. But then she looked up at him and pointed to the white sheet of paper.

She had printed,
HERE DAVID⟶
She then took the piece of paper and held it so that
the arrow pointed to the magazine picture of a tall blond
boy.

John smiled and said, "It does look like him. Yes, it
does, Lisa."

She snatched the paper back, turned it over, and
printed,
MURIEL
MURIEL
She then gave it back to John.

"All right, Muriel."

She took the piece of paper back and printed,
MURIEL—LISA—MURIEL. She smiled at him.

He said nothing and smiled back.

*

"A clock is to tell time. You know, twelve o'clock,
two—Say, do you know about numbers? Did they teach
you about numbers in that school?"

She wrote, 1 2 3 4 5.

"That's right. Very good—very good, indeed. You
apparently know more than you let on."

David spent the next half-hour drawing clock faces
and teaching her how to tell time. Even he was surprised
at the rapidity with which she learned. However, when
he became philosophical about time, telling about it as
a dimension and discussing its importance, she lost interest and no longer paid attention. After a while she
left, to look for John. When she found him, she drew

48

clocks for him and demonstrated her newfound knowledge.

David went off to play chess but couldn't find the
boy he had played with. He went to Alan's office and
told him that he couldn't find his chess partner. Alan
suggested that they play a game together, and they did.
After the sixth move it became apparent that David was
in control of the game.

"Are you letting me win?"

"Letting you? Indeed not."

"Are you sure? You know, part of the therapeutic
approach—Getting-to-know-you-better kind of rot—plus,
Make the kid feel good."

"You are suspicious; but let me tell you, as I did once
before, I have not and will not manipulate you in any
way whatsoever."

"I don't know about me being suspicious. But it
seems—well, you're not playing too well."

"Now, let's get this straight. I play chess with you as
I would with anybody. I have too much respect for you
to play down in any way. I am playing my best. Did it
ever occur to you that you're just a better chess player
than I am?"

David smiled. "Me better than you? Well, seems
funny."

"Doesn't seem funny to me. I may be older and more
expert in psychiatry—after all, I've studied it for years
—but you undoubtedly are better versed in other things
than I am."

"You're trying to make me feel good."

"Not at all. If you feel good, I'm glad for you. But

I am simply stating a fact. The fact is you know more about physics than I do, certainly more about horology. I know more medicine—more psychiatry. All of us, you know, have different assets, abilities, and educations."

"Let's play chess."

"OK."

They made two more moves. David now had him in an impossible position. Another move and Alan would be set up for the checkmate.

David got up. "Well, that's enough. Have some work to do in the library."

"Just a minute." Alan reached up.

"Don't touch me!"

"I won't—but we're close to the end; why not finish?"

"What for? It's—well, it's late."

"David, are you afraid—afraid of beating me? We'll still be friends, you know. It's only a chess game. I've lost before."

He sat down and said nothing. In two more moves he mated him.

"Good game, David. I really enjoyed it."

"But you lost."

"I would get a kick out of winning—but you know something?—the real kick is in playing—especially with a good player who can teach me a thing or two. Now, how about some lunch?"

"I am hungry."

They left for the dining room—together.

*

MURIEL   MURIEL   MURIEL, she printed.

"What about Muriel?" John asked.

MURIEL MURIEL

LISA
"Yes, yes," John said eagerly.
MURIEL—LISA—SAME

M   E

"Yes. All you—that's true."
But she got up and ran off to the other side of the room.

For a minute she stared at Alan and David, who were talking, but then got bored and went to look at some magazines.

*

"Clocks are more interesting than people."
"How so?"
"They're more accurate, more predictable, and just plain more interesting."
"They're more intricate."
"Clocks?"
"No, people."
"Well, I don't know. Some of these timepieces—but—" He smiled. "Yes, I must admit the human mechanism is more complicated."
"It is—but that's largely because it is not a mechanism. It is not an it; it is a he or she—a person."
"A person. So—what are you getting at?"
"A person. You're right—not predictable because not mechanical. A person—human."

"Human? What's 'human' supposed to encompass?"

"Well—human being—feeling—changing and being unpredictable."

"What's so hot about that?"

"Hot, cold—we are what we are—humans, not clocks."

"A clock is still easier to cope with."

"David, perhaps you are afraid of people?"

"Afraid of people? I suppose so—and perhaps with good reason, too!"

"When you trust yourself more, you'll be less afraid of other people, too."

"Words—just words."

"I don't think so."

He got up and went to his room. He studied the clock plans—but kept thinking of the conversation he had with Alan.

A week later he sat with Alan. For a while he said nothing, but after about ten minutes he spoke.

"I thought about it."

"About what?"

"Me. You know, being afraid of people."

"Yes."

"Well, I think—well, I am afraid—but I'm still interested in clocks and time and things."

"They're not mutually exclusive."

"Meaning what?"

"Meaning, you can still be interested in clocks—just for their own sake."

"But what about death?"

"What about it?"

"Well, I admit it—I'm afraid of it."

"Must be a relief to admit it."

"Yes, I think it is. But isn't everyone afraid of it?"

"Not everyone—but lots of people—to a lesser or greater degree."

"Lesser, greater?"

"Well, my feeling is that people who are afraid to live are afraid to die."

"You mean, if you do a lot of living—then you haven't missed much when you die."

"More or less."

"You know, I just remembered something."

"What's that?"

"I remember going into a movie. I was thirteen years old; it was a bright, sunny day. The movie was dark, pitch black. I found a seat—away—away from everybody. I sat and watched the movie for a while. Suddenly I had a terrible feeling; I broke into a sweat—my heart beat wildly. What I thought of was being dead—the world being there and me gone. The feeling was awful; I felt like I was losing myself—like I was disappearing. Then I ran out of the blackness of the movie into the sunlight. As soon as I got out into the light I felt better."

"You hadn't disappeared."

"No," he said solemnly. "I was still there."

"What were you watching when the fright began?"

"I don't know. You know, I thought about it many times but could never remember. It's funny—my memory is nearly perfect—but that—I couldn't remember."

"I see."

"I'll tell you something I do remember."

"What's that?"

"Well—about a year after that movie incident—I figured something out."

"Yes?"

"I figured out that in a way we never die at all."

"How's that?"

"Well, if people have children and children have children—in a way we go on living just like the branches of a tree."

"It's a very interesting thought."

"Interesting? Well, I don't know. But this I know: at times thinking about it in this way makes me feel lots better."

"Good."

"There's Lisa; I'll see you later."

"OK."

*

"What do you think about what I told you last week?"

"What are you referring to?"

"Oh, you know—my fears. You know, all that pathology."

"Pathology?"

"Yes—my being afraid of death, and of people."

"Well, its being pathological or nonpathological is not terribly important."

"Not important! It's important enough to be keeping me here."

"While that's true, I'm still not terribly interested in your fears pathologically. Setting judgments—sick, sicker; pathological—it's not too important."

"Then what is?"

54

"Your fears are symptoms—and also symbols. As such they have value—value as routes to what it is that generated them in the first place."

"I see."

"Do you?" Alan smiled.

"Yes, I think I do—but—well, you're so bland. So—well, isn't it unusual to be so accepting of such sickness—of being crazy?"

"Bland, unusual—words, only words. This I can tell you: only by accepting our difficulties can we use them to better understand ourselves—and to grow healthier. Calling ourselves names—crazy and so forth—it just doesn't serve any purpose."

"Healthier, that's a laugh."

"No, it's not a laugh. Let me tell you, everybody—no matter how sick—also has much health, too."

"You mean a combination?"

"Exactly."

"Even me?"

"Most certainly you."

"You know, it just occurred to me."

"What's that?"

"Your name and mine are colors. Alan White, David Green—White and Green."

"That's true; I hadn't thought of it either."

They sat a while and said nothing. After five minutes, David spoke. "The other day there was something I remembered that I wanted to tell you."

"Oh?"

"Yes. I sat here with you and kept thinking about it—but couldn't talk about it."

"Oh, that will happen—and perhaps one day, when you're ready, you'll talk about it."

That night before he went to bed, he thought about it again.

He was eleven and went to a freak show. He saw a boy who was supposed to be turning into an elephant but that didn't bother him. Then he saw a man who put needles through his skin, and he didn't like that at all. At another platform he saw a dwarfed, hunchbacked man billed as "The Human Frog," and he felt terribly sorry for him. Then he came to Alan-Adele—half-man, half-woman. He looked, fascinated—one side bearded, the other side smooth-shaved; flat-chested and full-breasted; short hair, long hair. Then he made the error; he thought of himself. He became terrified and ran out of the show shaking and sweating. He still felt odd when he thought about it. But he couldn't talk about the memory to anybody. Not yet.

*

He decided to try it. He would not rhyme; he would talk to her straight. He sat in the day room in a large rocking chair. A few other patients came in and walked about, but they ignored each other. John came in and said, "Hello," but David did not reply. It was raining outside, a heavy spring rain, but the room was large and bright, well lighted, with many pictures. He looked out the window, at the rain—and the picture of a big beach umbrella popped into his mind. Then he thought of his mother's diaphragm. It was well hidden, and he came

56

across it by accident. He had heard about condoms and thought this was one. It had been in one of their secret places. He didn't touch it—just looked. It seemed all rolled up. But its diameter, its circumference, was huge. He would never grow into the size of that. He remembered running out of the room.

Just then Lisa came in. She immediately walked over to him. John sat at the other side of the room and read the newspaper.

"David, David, how are you? It's raining out—what shall we do?"

"It would have been nice to walk in the garden. But we will do it another time. Come sit down in the chair —over here." He pointed at the other rocker.

She looked at him quizzically. She had rhymed—and he hadn't.

"Chair, there," she whispered, and sat down.

"Lisa, it's hard for me to rhyme. Listen to me—even if it's plain—straight. Lisa, stay." He spoke very slowly and carefully. Now he hesitated—then said, "Lisa, trust me."

She looked up into his eyes. She looked startled and afraid. Then she said in a deeper voice than usual, "David, David, your face is nice; soft, soft—not like snow, not like ice."

He smiled. They sat in the room and rocked up and back in the chairs.

*

"David, hello, you look nice."
"So do you, Lisa."

"Today I'm fifteen, David—fifteen. Let's go and look out the window."

"Happy birthday, Lisa. Lisa, you're not talking in rhymes." His heart beat wildly; then he whispered, "And you're not writing. You're you—Lisa, not Muriel."

"Lisa, Muriel, different, the same—just names. Let's look out the window."

He became very pale and he trembled, and his breathing became quicker and deeper. "Lisa." He swallowed hard. "Lisa, take my hand."

She looked up into his eyes and slowly took his hand.

He stiffened and felt a surge of fright course from his hand through the rest of his body. He clenched his teeth, and tears ran down his cheeks, but he hadn't died.

Hand in hand, they walked to the window.

NOTES

Lisa Brent

Initial Intake Note

September 15, 1958

This thirteen-year-old white girl initially appears about two or three years younger than her stated age. Physical examination, however, reveals a normally developed thirteen-year-old, menarche having commenced at age eleven.

Age—13
Height—5' 4"
Weight—98
Blood pressure—100/70
Pulse—76
Respiration—Normal
Temperature—98.7
Blood Study—Negative

Skin reveals no stigmata.
Eye, ear, nose, and throat
  are normal
Heart, lungs, and abdomen
  are normal.
Extremities are normal.
Urine Analysis—Negative
Chest X-ray—Normal

Neuromuscular reflexes are slightly exaggerated but are within normal limits. Neurologic examination—including response to light, touch, heat, cold, pain; hearing, seeing; and fundi examination—is negative.

In conclusion, there is no evidence of system pathology. Neurologic, respiratory, circulatory, digestive, and urinary examination reveals no demonstrable lesion.

PSYCHIATRIC EXAMINATION   Lisa is a tall, thin, dark-complexioned child. Her eyes are large and light brown; her nose is short and straight. She has a small mouth and even white teeth. Her straight brown hair is parted on the side and is usually disheveled and occasionally neat. Lisa's expression, appearance, and the impression she makes are more than ordinarily linked to fluctuations in her mood and personality. She is about four-fifths of the time a pixie-looking, eye-darting, disorganized, hyperactive four-year-old. She darts about the room, hopping, skipping, and jumping—at times in a dystonic fashion, feet and arms disorganized and going in all directions, and at other times skipping and jumping with the precision of a practiced athlete. In this identity she calls herself Lisa, fluctuates from poor to fair contact, and speaks only in rhymes—in a high, sing-song, infantile voice. Occasionally she moves about in a sluggish fashion, appearing depressed. During these usually brief periods her eyes change from a darting near-squint to a wide-eyed expression of dreaminess and pathos. The observer was surprised during observation of the first of the latter moods at the unusual size of her eyes.

About one-fifth of the time Lisa's identity, mood, and activity become radically changed. Her psychomotor activity becomes markedly reduced. She walks about in ladylike fashion, almost gracefully. The pixie quality disappears, as does the affective impression of seeming to be a very young child. There is no longer evidence of giggling and silliness. Lisa then appears to be her stated age. However, she no longer calls herself Lisa. At this time she becomes "Muriel," a name which often comes up in her rhymes as Lisa. During the Muriel identification the patient is mute, but she can write, a skill learned in the A—— School prior to her admission here. When given pencil and paper, she may or may not print a few words. Her printing and language are surprisingly good, but we feel that she has even better potential. As Lisa, she is aware of her Muriel characteristics. We suspect that she is aware of Lisa as Muriel—but not as aware. Is it possible that her antics as Lisa embarrass her?

There is undoubtedly considerable autistic preoccupation, but at present it is not possible to expose or to evaluate it.

Attention span is extremely poor, making testing almost impossible. From her rhyming productions, however, we can ascertain good orientation in place and person (Lisa/Muriel). We cannot evaluate her orientation in time. From her rhymes, printing, and previous testing we suspect the existence of a superior I.Q. and considerable talent. There are no demonstrable hallucinatory experiences; however, their existence would not be surprising. Aside from the Muriel delusion and preoccupation, there is no evidence of delusional production.

From observation and the small amount of testing possible, we discern much underlying anxiety. To ward off panic attacks, which occur infrequently, she obviously defends herself with hyperactivity, rhyming, disassociation, and mutism. The hyperactivity probably serves to rid her of the excess energy of her anxiety. The rhyming may be a way of repressing certain affects by a veneer of silliness or nursery-rhyming activity but at the same time managing to communicate. Now these affects may be bound up in the compartment labeled "Muriel." The mutism of Muriel may be a last-ditch attempt to repress threatening displays of unwanted feelings. Of course, the latter explanations are only speculations, which will or will not be substantiated only after much time has passed.

From the history and the small amount of testing and contact possible, we feel that Lisa is having much difficulty with the upsurge of sexual feeling and affect in general, particularly anger. Her sickness is essentially an attempt to cope with the latter uncontrollable feelings.

DIAGNOSTIC DISCUSSION The patient projects a general feeling characteristic of hebephrenia. The giggling, sil-

61

liness, autistic preoccupation, and affective display of a much younger age level—all contribute to that picture.

However, while her rhymes are sometimes irrational and characteristic of a thought disorder, they are more often rational and indicate a relatively good ability to communicate. There is seldom evidence of a word salad. This, plus the presence of a disassociative process, detracts from that diagnosis.

Suffice to say, then, that the patient is a very sick little girl presenting elements characteristic of hebephrenic schizophrenia complicated by an ability to disassociate, characteristic of multiple personality.

PROGNOSIS   Very serious in view of present findings and their duration, which is dated from at least age six.

RECOMMENDATION   Continuous relating treatment with a therapist—not necessarily a psychiatrist—and maximum freedom, including mixing with one or two other children in the day room.

Six-Month Interval Note

March 15, 1959

The patient's relationship to her therapist and to other patients remains completely superficial and paltry. There have been no changes in her productions or general behavior pattern.

No discernible progress can be noted.

SIX-MONTH INTERVAL NOTE

September 15, 1959

The patient is beginning to relate simultaneously to another patient—David Green—and to her therapist. Her rhyming productions are directed toward them, as is a considerable portion of her interest. There is no other great change in her productivity or general behavior pattern.

ONE-YEAR SUMMARY NOTE

September 15, 1960

There have been some significant changes during the last twelve-month period. Testing is still not possible. Her writing ability is definitely improved.

Lisa has continued to relate to David Green (see notes on David Green) and the relationship has become less superficial. This has apparently led to a more solidified transference to her therapist, with whom she spends more time and to whom she is more communicative. Her attention span has increased, and it is now possible to discern good orientations in time. There is less hyperactivity, giggling, and silliness. Her disassociative activity seems to be diminished. The compartmentalization of Lisa/Muriel is becoming more fluid. Though she still uses both names, Muriel comes up more frequently in the Lisa rhymes and Lisa in her Muriel printing. It is not possible to determine the degree or significance of an integrative process at this time. It should be noted, however, that on at least one occasion Lisa and Muriel became one, and the patient spoke without rhyming.

Her rhyming activity has undergone a significant transition. Her rhyming two years ago consisted of nonsense syllables meaningful only to herself and was full of neologisms and clang formations. The rhymings at this time were largely primitive productions of primary process and mainly autistic formulations. At times the productions were jumbled enough to be considered a word salad not unlike that of classic hebephrenia. About a year ago her rhyming underwent a more and more pronounced change. It seldom resembled a word salad and began to make much sense. It lost much of the neologic formation and began to deal less with autistic material and more with environmental properties. In short, it changed from a primary-process phenomenon to a secondary-process one. It dealt less with her inner world and more with the outer one she lives in. Her rhymings more and more became comments on things going on about her. The third and final phase of the rhyming transition occurred during this last year and has become more developed during the last six months. This phase has largely consisted of using the rhymes to communicate—to talk to both John and David. An obviously increased desire to talk with David and her therapist has made it more difficult to rhyme. Perhaps a combination of things is taking place. Perhaps her increased trust in herself plus the desire to talk are leading to loosening of the rhyming defense.

Despite obvious progress, the patient continues to be hyperactive, continues to rhyme, continues to be autistic at times, continues to disassociate (though diminished),

64

and in general continues to be extremely immature. She also continues to demonstrate inappropriate affect— thought not as inappropriate as on admission. She continues to be fearful, at times hiding in closets for long periods.

PROGNOSIS   In view of duration and intensity of illness, prognosis, while brighter, remains very serious.

RECOMMENDATION   Continued institutionalization and continued relating therapy.

David Green

INITIAL INTAKE NOTE

September 15, 1958

This fifteen-year-old white boy appears to be about his stated age. Physical examination reveals a tall, thin, normally developed fifteen-year-old.

Age—15	Blood Study—Negative
Height—5′ 10″	Urine Analysis—Normal
Weight—131	Chest X-ray—Normal
Blood Pressure—110/76	Skin reveals no stigmata.
Pulse—70	Eyes—myopic, moderate.
Respiration—Normal	Ears, nose, and throat are
Temperature—98.6	normal.
	Extremities are normal.

Neurologic examination—including neuromuscular reflexes; response to light, touch, cold, heat, pain; hearing, seeing; and fundi examination—is negative.

In conclusion, there is no evidence of system pathology. Neurologic, respiratory, circulatory, digestive, and urinary examination reveals no demonstrable lesion.

PSYCHIATRIC EXAMINATION This is a tall, small-boned, narrow-shouldered, white boy, who appears to be approximately his stated age. His hair is straight, dark blond, and perfectly parted on the side. His eyes are large, light blue, and sleepy-looking. His skin is light and clear, his mouth small, teeth even, and nose straight and fine. His features are regular and in good proportion to one another, but his face seems small for his body and has a pinched quality. David is always dressed completely and immaculately in either a gray tweed or blue serge suit, white shirt, and matching tie. His black shoes shine faultlessly, and his socks are held high by garters. He wears brown horn-rimmed glasses.

He speaks in a low, well-modulated voice, often with obvious if not blatant sarcasm, at other times with only a suggestion of sarcasm and bitterness. His pronunciation is excellent—each word being enunciated with precise clarity. His characteristic precision of speech seems to be effortless and probably a habit of long standing.

The patient is well oriented in all spheres and does not demonstrate overt evidence of hallucinating phenomena. His memory is excellent, and his vocabulary extensive. I.Q. is extremely high. The patient enters interview situations and psychologic testing reluctantly. There is sufficient cooperation, however, to glean considerable information. During interviews the patient demonstrates considerable controlled hostility, which

66

makes itself felt by sarcasm and an occasional muffled outburst of anger. Affect is appropriate for the most part. There is, however, some flattening, best demonstrated in areas where considerably less emotion is expressed than would be expected. There is enormous arrogance, and a thin veneer of superiority, undoubtedly evidence of extreme underlying fragility and fear of emotional contact. The patient had become increasingly seclusive and fearful up until the time of his present admission. The latter seclusiveness and fear continue.

The patient is phobic about bodily contact. He cannot tolerate being touched. Physical examination was very difficult, David having insisted on placing the stethoscope, diaphragm, etc., himself. The latter condition has existed for at least five years and has increased in intensity in the last few months prior to entrance at this institution. At present this phobia borders on the delusional, inasmuch as the patient feels that touching may result in death.

David is obsessed with cleanliness, neatness, logic, and precision. A specific obsession involves time and timekeeping mechanisms. He spends many hours drawing clocks and watches and during interviewing expressed much preoccupation with time.

He has good abstraction ability but unexpectedly tends to become concrete intermittently. This concrete approach is mainly expressed in an attempt to mechanize much of his thinking. When he does become involved in discussion, he intellectualizes a great deal and in general impresses the examiner with much overintellectualization. He undoubtedly spends much of his time secluded and preoccupied in autistic activity. While he will discuss general issues, physics, math, clocks, time, and some philosophy, he remains detached and alienated when discussing himself, absolutely refusing to describe early memories, relationships, or his family. Attempts at such discussion result in circumstantiality and evasiveness. Despite some apparent intellectual insight as regards his condition and admission here, insight on any deeper level—that is, on an emotional level—is remarkably lacking. There are well-guarded manifestations of paranoid ideation, but no evidence of a thought disorder other than extreme fear of bodily contact and time-clock preoccupation. Attention span in contact with interviewers is only fair; therefore, a number of short interviews were used to elicit the latter material.

While the patient did permit psychologic testing, cooperation was at best limited. He was sarcastic, resentful, bored, and restless. Nevertheless, there were enough Rorschach and T.A.T. responses to permit some theoretical conclusions. He found I.Q. testing more tolerable and at times seemed involved and even interested.

I.Q. is above 145. General knowledge is extensive and characteristic of a much older individual. However, despite the great fund of general knowledge, a naivete characteristic of a much younger child is always in evidence. The patient demonstrates considerable narcissistic preoccupation and much infantile omnipotence. Identity is poor, as is self-esteem, with much evidence of fragility and a great fund of self-doubt. There is much underlying anxiety and anger, and a very poor ability to accept and to handle these. General fearfulness and preoccupation with death are evident throughout, as is

68

fear of people and relationships of even a superficial nature. There is evidence of sexual upsurgence and an intense effort at control, repression, and denial. There is also much sexual confusion, especially as regards his own sexual identity, which is very poorly established. The patient is extremely defensive, and his defenses for the most part follow an obsessive-compulsive pattern with a definite tendency toward paranoid ideation. While responses and general ideation are not typically characteristic of schizophrenia, they are nevertheless quite florid and at times very bizarre. This is especially true when his anger is tapped. There is also evidence of considerable hopelessness and underlying depression, undoubtedly a function of much self-hate and degradation. There is an unusual degree of cynicism in one so young.

DIAGNOSTIC DISCUSSION   The patient has suffered from a multitude of neurotic symptoms during a majority of his young life. While the predominant symptomatic thread is characteristic of an obsessive-compulsive neurosis, there are sufficient other symptoms (phobias, anxiety attacks) to warrant a diagnosis of neurotic reaction, chronic *mixed* type. However, there is also evidence of graver pathology. There is much basic anxiety, poor identification, especially in the sexual area, much self-hate, poor relatedness, and bizarre Rorschach responses, all of which makes us think seriously of a diagnosis of pseudo-neurotic schizophrenia. In any case, we are dealing with a very fragile, anxiety-ridden, adolescent boy, who, defense-wise, is treading the line between neurosis and psychosis and who, despite great intelligence, is at present almost nonfunctional. The diagnosis of mixed neurosis with possible schizophrenic underpinnings will be retained for the time being.

PROGNOSIS   Serious.

RECOMMENDATION   The patient will be allowed as much freedom as possible and will be seen in psychotherapy, as willing, with Dr. Alan White.

SIX-MONTH INTERVAL NOTE

March 15, 1959

The patient remains seclusive, spending almost all of his time alone, with books. His motivation in treatment has been very poor. Instead of regular sessions, Dr. White has made himself available at any time and has spent time in the day room with him. However, David speaks to him only infrequently and for a few minutes at a time.

SIX-MONTH INTERVAL NOTE

September 15, 1959

David has become slightly more communicative, occasionally returning the greeting of other patients and staff members.

He seems to be interested in Lisa Brent, at least superficially, observing her and trying to talk to her. He is also spending more time with Dr. White.

He is making more use of the library and day room.

70

One-Year Summary Note

September 15, 1960

At the beginning of this period David became interested in Lisa Brent on what he claimed was an intellectual, clinical basis. This apparently changed to an emotional relationship. He has spent increasing time with her, and there has been communication between them. He has even allowed himself to be touched by her on at least one occasion. He has also played chess with another patient, has become less seclusive, and spends time in the day room.

There has been at the same time increased interest in sessions with Dr. White and the establishment of a fairly strong positive transference.

In treatment it is obvious that he is emotionally involved with Lisa and has focused some of his externalizations and paranoid process on Lisa's therapist, probably a function of his jealousy and possessiveness. He has become less arrogant, less sarcastic, and less intellectualized. There is also evidence of less autistic preoccupation, with great interest in himself in relation to Dr. White and the rest of the world. He has also begun to repress less, bringing up emotionally laden early memories. He does not speak of his family, however, and Dr. White has not pressed for such productions. Dr. White has likewise not touched any of his neurotic defenses (phobias, fears, or externalizations). David has also steered clear of sexual subjects, though his therapist feels that there are undoubtedly sexual feelings for Lisa present. His dreams have become less bizarre and less replete with anger and murder. In general, there is less fear of anger. Anger toward his doctor is now expressed with affect rather than as superior, intellectual statements. The patient seems more hopeful and, interestingly enough, has begun to ask for reassurance as to the possibility of growth and change.

Rorschach demonstrates slightly less bizarreness in the quality of the responses and somewhat less confusion as regards identity sexually. There is still considerable anxiety and anger, and a tendency toward paranoid ideation. There is still considerable infantilism and naivete.

Compulsive cleanliness, fear of body contact, and for the most part detachment from other people continue. The obsession with clocks and time persists, but to a lesser degree. Intellectualization also persists, but to a lesser degree.

PROGNOSIS   In view of obvious progress especially as regards emotional involvement with another child and his therapist, prognosis is improved. David seems to be veering away from the borderline of schizophrenia. However, in view of long history and seriousness of illness, prognosis must still remain guarded.

RECOMMENDATION   Continued institutionalization here and treatment with Dr. White. If improvement continues, discharge from the institution and treatment with Dr. White outside may be possible in the next six months to a year. It must be remembered that David is still anxiety-ridden and many months away from the time when he will be able to become involved in the problems of his neurotic defenses, sexuality, and family relations.

72

II

From childhood's hour I have not been
As others were—I have not seen
As others saw.
— EDGAR ALLAN POE

What happens to a dream deferred?
— LANGSTON HUGHES

Winter:1985

H E read the letter. Actually, it was a note. Only a line.

David, I would like to see you.
Lisa

*

He stared out the bay window. He thought, How fast the mountains change when the summer is finally over.

He reread the note several times. But it disclosed nothing more. For the first time in a long while he felt disquietude, and though he wasn't fully aware of it, the feeling was composed of happy excitement and apprehension.

*

The Berkshires in the winter are cold, bleak—and beautiful to those who enjoy low clouds and firelit, snug rooms. Many of the large frame houses are more than one hundred and fifty years old. Their rooms are relatively small, and their ceilings were built low in order to conserve heat. Some have wonderful wood-paneled walls, expertly crafted heavy doors, and large fireplaces that can be sat in by even two people at a time. There are a number of bay windows, and many of the other windows are multipaneled into small squares.

The school, a treatment and educational center for adolescents with somewhat more than the usual emotional problems, sits on the site of an old farm. Some of the buildings have been renovated, and there have been additions to accommodate classrooms, a library, craft rooms, kitchens, dining rooms, a large social hall, an infirmary, offices, and several other spaces necessary for this kind of place. A few of the old farmhouses are still intact. Students live in some, and the staff live in the others.

The place is financially well endowed, and individual attention and treatment is commonplace. There are never more than sixty student patients in residence. The staff is relatively small but select. The farm is large for an institution of this size, stretching over more than twenty-five acres of hilly land. Some of it, around the main buildings, is cleared. The rest is wooded.

Most of the buildings are three floors high, and the mountains can be seen from almost all the doors and windows, especially those on the upper two stories.

The school is just about equidistant from the several Berkshire towns and is therefore a considerable distance from all of them. It is almost self-sufficient, and its distance from other farms, houses, and the towns makes for enough of a sense of isolation to make it feel like a tiny village in the mountains.

But it is comforting, should the winter become oppressive, to know that Stockbridge (quaint and charming), Great Barrington (a solid "blue-collar farm town"), Lenox (beautiful, old Lenox), and even the small city of Pittsfield aren't that far off.

76

Indoors, the air often smells of cedar and pine cones burning in the fireplace and food cooking in the kitchen. Outdoors, the air is clear, clean, and sharp. Often, it all combines to add to the special mood of the place, which people enjoy, mostly without conscious awareness of the ingredients.

*

They were in David's office, really a small, comfortable sitting room, rather spare and neat but informal. There was no desk—a table with papers, pencils, and pens neatly arranged against the wall and a chair. There were a few nice paintings of farmhouses and mountains on the paneled walls. The fire seemed to be going out in the fireplace, but there was an occasional pop from the embers, still red.

It was four in the afternoon, almost dark out—just enough light to see that the snow had not yet started. But it was there in the heavy clouds, and the temperature was right for it.

The boy's name was Bob Mathis. He was sixteen, quite tall, about six-two, and very thin. He actually weighed one hundred forty-five pounds and ate well but remained painfully "skinny" as he thought of himself. Bob had high cheekbones and a rather sharp, jutting chin. Everything about him seemed angular to David. His eyes were gray, his hair a sandy brown. His mouth had a tight, pinched quality, but this disappeared when at rare times he laughed and showed even white teeth.

David was handsome when he was Bob's age and he was handsome as a grown man. There were streaks of gray in his blond hair, but he looked at least five years younger than forty-two. David was about six feet tall, slim, and had a tennis player look of fitness, though he hardly participated in any physical activity other than long walks. His eyes were light blue and more than usually alert. He was prone to half-smiles, which added to his charm and considerable charisma. But the overall effect of his face was that of sensitivity and vulnerability, mostly conveyed by eyes and mouth.

Both man and boy were dressed in well-matched trousers, sport jackets, and ties and conveyed a strong impression of neatness. This was further emphasized by the way the other people at the school, both staff and students, dressed. Everyone else nearly always wore the most casual clothes, and more than a few could even be called sloppy.

They sat in comfortable easy chairs semifacing each other.

"Kids say you went to school here." This said as an almost offhand side remark of no importance.

"I did," David answered.

"So you were nuts too?"

"Could say that," David answered evenly.

After a minute the boy said sadly now, "I guess you never left here."

"Not true," David answered quickly and thought, I sound defensive, and was slightly annoyed with himself. But he found himself going on even as he believed he ought to keep quiet and just listen.

"I went to college. Then to medical school," and after a pause he added, "hospitals."

Bob pounced on the last word. "Hospitals!"

78

"To train!" David answered quickly—too quickly—defensively, he thought.

"You mean to learn to train us," Bob said sourly. David ignored the remark. Mournfully now, Bob said, "You came back here. You were out there and you came back."

"I knew I would all along."

"Why?" And after a few seconds he asked again, "Why?" This time almost imploringly.

"Lots of reasons," David shrugged and half-smiled. But Bob didn't let it go.

"Couldn't make it on the outside?" Bob asked sympathetically.

"You're wrong," David answered at once—firmly and calmly—but defensive again, he thought, going on, "I did make it on the outside. I told you I worked in hospitals. I thought it was more important to make it here. I was more drawn to—to—this kind of work."

Neither of them said anything for several minutes. David felt that the session had not gone well. He asked himself what Bob was saying—really saying—and then he tried to regain control and make it worthwhile after all.

"Sounds like you want to promote your hopelessness."

"Why would I want to do that?" Bob asked, genuinely puzzled.

"Perhaps to stay here. Maybe deep down you want to make sure you never have to leave here."

Bob immediately changed the subject.

"You'll take over when Alan dies?"

For a second David looked angry, but quickly composed himself and said carefully and calmly, "Alan is fine, and I'm not taking over anything," and thought, He's resistant and I'm defensive.

Bob had left. David sat in the chair at the table. He read the letter again. He said out loud, "David Shmavid." He examined the envelope. Instead of a return address there was a telephone number. The prefix was 203. He knew it was a Connecticut number.

"I never left here," he said out loud to himself.

*

Alan White was over sixty. The fringe of hair around his otherwise bald head was gray. He was thin now. But his clothes, including a cashmere coat-sweater, hung loose, giving evidence of recent weight loss. His color was poor. He seemed fragile. But his face had residual strength, and his voice was deep and resonant. His hazel eyes were sad. He had a generous mouth and smiled readily. His movements were smoother and more certain than those of an old man, but they were slow and somewhat careful and he tended to speak that way too.

They were in Alan's office, best described as a casual, small library. There were books all over the place—on an old oak desk, on built-in shelves, on a large architect's table, on a couch. It was an eclectic collection—history, philosophy, religion, anthropology, novels old and new, biography, psychiatry, and a dozen psychiatric and psychoanalytic journals. The only books lined up in perfect order in a small freestanding old glass-doored mahogany bookcase were twenty-seven volumes of Freud's work, translated and edited by James Strachey; Freud's book on the interpretation of dreams; his biography in three volumes, by Ernest Jones; and five works of Karen Horney and her biography, by Jack Rubins.

David, dressed neatly as usual, sat slouched down on the Victorian couch, legs stretched forward on the floor. Alan sat in a large upholstered wing chair sipping tea. He was a tea addict, and this was the one habit he could not break despite an otherwise almost flawless compliance with his doctor's directions. He had had a serious myocardial infarction eighteen months earlier.

They both seemed very comfortable, quite relaxed.

David said, "Twenty-five years."

"I know," Alan replied.

"Perhaps I should just ignore it."

"Can you?" Alan asked gently.

"No," he answered in an unmistakably resigned tone.

"Have you thought about her through the years?" This asked by Alan—slowly, carefully.

"Every day," David answered, and there was that wistful half-smile, but then he was all business and asked, "How sick was she when she finally left?"

"You know how sick."

"But she was here five years more after I left."

"You read my notes on her?" Still gently and carefully.

"Then you know she was much better—but," and Alan shrugged.

"What a specialty," David nodded, and the half-smile was there again.

"Complaints?" Alan smiled too.

"There's always the *buts*—the trailing off—the uncertainty. An ophthalmologist examines a patient who can't see. She has a cataract. He operates. The patient can see. No strings! Cured—definitively!"

"Not the same, and you know it," Alan said good-naturedly and then added seriously, "It's all strings with us, all loose ends. Life is all loose ends. All of it is unfinished business."

"You recommended treatment when she left?" David's legs were no longer sprawled out. He was hunched over, his elbows on his knees, his head resting on his hands. They no longer seemed relaxed.

"Yes."

"Did she see someone outside?"

"Yes." And then Alan added carefully, "Still does maybe."

"Then you've heard from her all these years." David sat upright eagerly now.

"No." Alan then added quickly, "I spoke to her therapist now and then—the man I recommended."

"So you know she's in Connecticut and you know how she is."

"No!" Alan replied quickly, "Matter of fact he's in New York. Is she in Connecticut? I haven't talked to him in at least five years."

"What did he tell you then?"

"Only that she was all right. Nothing more."

"Another virtue of our business," David said bitterly.

Alan raised his eyebrows.

"Secrecy unto foolishness."

Alan ignored the remark.

"I didn't know she never left your mind."

"I know," and he flopped back on the couch, legs stretched out again.

Alan hesitated and then asked, "Would it be easier to see her here? I mean, that is—if you want to see her."

"Here?" David asked, sitting up again.

"Maybe during Christmas—she could stay at our house. I'm sure it would be fine with Betty."

After a prolonged silence David, crouched over again, his head in his hands, said, "I'm afraid."

"I know," Alan sighed.

*

Unlike other Connecticut towns, Rowayton is neither posh nor industrial. In some ways it is not unlike old Provincetown on Cape Cod. Its main street runs perpendicular to the beach area and parallel to a large boat basin mostly full of small sailing and motor boats. There are small, charming stores, but art galleries have not flourished here.

The people are a mix of business executives, journalists, publishers, musicians, latter-day bohemians, writers, actors, advertising people, and there is an artist's colony. The colony has no center, so the artists live in various parts of the village or a bit beyond its immediate borders.

Many of the people live in this small community because they want or need to be close to New York as well as to water, space, light, and sky in order to paint or just to sit or walk.

The most expensive houses border the beach and Long Island Sound—the vast stretch of water that separates Connecticut from Long Island and eventually joins the white water of the ocean.

Lisa's house, like many in Rowayton, is similar to the

smaller, old New England houses of the Berkshires and Massachusetts.The house is a very long walk from the beach, but it sits on a hill and has a water view from many of its windows.

Lisa shares the house and expenses with her friends, Jean and Tom Martin. They also share the large studio, which occupies the entire third and highest floor.

They are artists, and their paintings have sold, have been exhibited in good galleries, and have been reviewed, sometimes favorably in significant publications. But their expenses are steadily paid by commercial assignments from advertising agencies, magazines, department stores, and publishers. Lisa's specialty has been book jackets. They have kept themselves on a free-lance basis and have limited their assignments so as to have time for serious painting. Sometimes one gets in the way of the other, largely because a creative urge or flow can rarely be willed to conform to a practical schedule.

*

Jean Martin was about forty and looked her age. She was tall, thin, rangy, blond, blue-eyed, and had a large, straight nose and wide smile. She was not pretty, but her face was strong and good, and it felt good to be in her presence. She was large-boned, and when she moved her arms or legs, she almost always seemed purposeful and decisive.

Lisa was forty but looked several years younger. She had smooth olive skin and brown hair, full lips, a generous mouth, even white teeth, a small straight nose, well-defined eyebrows, high cheekbones, and very large almond-shaped, chocolate-brown eyes. Lisa was tall, though not as tall as Jean. She had fine bones.

Lisa was a beautiful woman, but lacked the air of feminine self-assurance some women as good-looking as her have. It was hard to draw away from her striking eyes, especially when she smiled, but it was the curve of her mouth and smooth skin that gave her a very soft quality.

Jean's voice was of a high register, but words and phrases nearly always came out firmly in decisive definition, connoting strength and conviction.

Lisa's voice was medium range, but at times of low volume, and her speech could be hesitant, often betraying uncertainty and even fragility. There were other times, though, when she sounded assertive and even aggressive for a short while.

They sat in the studio on hard-backed simple chairs, drinking coffee, facing the sound on that cloudy morning. They were dressed in dungarees and cotton shirts. Lisa wore a heavy wool sweater. She tended to be cold. They nearly always dressed casually.

"I'm afraid."

"Of what?" Jean asked firmly.

"I don't know why I did it."

Jean just looked at her for a moment. They were through with the coffee. She took the cups and brought them to a small table at the opposite end of the room and then returned and sat down again, this time moving the chair close and around to face Lisa.

"Going up there. Seeing him." Lisa shook her head.

"But you wanted to—you wrote him." Though they were almost the same age, Jean took Lisa's hand between hers as a mother would do to comfort a daughter.

"A crazy urge—impulse."

"Just an urge?" Jean asked gently.

"No."

"How did he sound?"

"Very nice. As always." She caught herself and said derisively now, "Always—that's almost funny. I haven't talked to him in a thousand years."

"He invited you up there. I'm sure he wants to see you."

"Truth is I never stopped thinking of him. Jim reminded me of him. But they were different," she hastened to reassure herself. "He saved my life. When he left, I thought—"

"What?" Jean pressed.

"That I would come apart again."

"And you?" Jean was very firm now and squeezed her hand hard. "Didn't you save him too?"

"I don't know. I suppose so. But he became a doctor—the psychiatrist."

"And you became an artist. What does all that mean? You were both sick then. You were both patients. He was not a doctor then. You were never his patient. You're not his patient now."

"I ought to leave it alone. Write and cancel." Then after a pause she went on rapidly, "He's nothing like James. He sounds older but gentle. He reminded me of calling him David Shmavid. You know I couldn't talk out of rhyme."

"I know. You told me."

86

"I reminded him of his calling me a pearl of a girl. I suppose it sounds silly."

"No. It sounds fine. What did he say?"

"He said that when he first came to the school, what started out as the worst time in his life turned into the best." She stopped for a moment and said, "I told him it was true for me too. But maybe that's it!"

"What?" Jean asked and let go of Lisa's hand.

"That I know it."

"It?"

"That there's no going back again. I mean to those times," she hesitated, "to those feelings."

"If you know that," Jean was New England firm now, "then seeing him ought to be safe enough."

But she didn't feel "safe." She tried to paint, and nothing came of it. Then she worked on a sketch for a book jacket, but her concentration lasted for only a few minutes.

She sat for a while alone and quiet. She pictured him then—those many years ago and in her mind thought of his current voice, his phone voice. But this made her anxious and she willed herself to stop.

*

"Do you think I was in love with her? All my failed relationships between then and now."

"I don't know." Alan sipped his tea. His color was somewhat better. "For me love has come to mean caring, really caring. Infatuation is something else. Though I'm not against—" he searched for the right words, "the chemistry either."

"Oh, I cared. The chemistry must have been there too. Infatuated then or infatuated later about then. I don't know. I was too sick to know then."

"Plenty of distortions take place through the years. Exaggerated feelings about the past."

"I was infatuated at least a few times since then. Some powerful attractions, but caring, really caring? I think I have to go back to her to feel that, sick as I was then."

"All sounds rather cerebral—intellectual."

"Perhaps, but it doesn't feel that way. My memory of her and the both of us, here, is anything but intellectual."

"What gets stirred up?"

"Safety!" David answered without hesitation. "Tenderness, too," he added, "but I felt safe." And then he sighed and said half-smiling, "Maybe I felt really cared about for the first time."

"Is that what really brought you back to work here —safety?"

"Partially, sure. Do doctors ever stop being patients? But it's more than that." He groped silently for the right words, but they didn't come readily. But he went on, "When those times here—with her—with you—turned good for me—when I came out of that terrible despair," and again he stopped to find words, "there was a warmth and snug, close feeling—a brightness I felt that I never felt before or after."

"Maybe you were in love with her."

"And yet I never tried to contact her after I left."

"Didn't want to spoil the effect?"

"Maybe. Too much feeling. Too much closeness. I

certainly worked on those in treatment after I left, and yet some things never go away."

"Residuals," Alan said.

"It was a long time before I contacted you."

"Could have been important to keep this door closed for a while so as to go on."

They were silent for a few minutes. Alan poured another cup of tea. David stood up and looked out the window. The snow had stopped but it was cloudy, and the fireplace logs were cold now.

"Loose ends?" Alan asked.

"You're right," David answered, going back to the couch. "Life is all loose ends."

"And unfinished business," Alan added.

"All the years of analysis. Treatment with you. Through college, medical school. And then still another analysis—the institute, a training analysis—and I'm as ambivalent as ever."

"Ambivalence is the human condition," Alan went on carefully and gently. "I finally learned there's nothing wrong about being in conflict. We're always pulled in opposite directions. It's appropriate to being human. Trouble is, we don't know it. We look for a smoothness that doesn't exist." And then as an afterthought, "Trick is to accept conflict. Do this or that and know that something has to be lost in any choice—a price must be paid."

David sighed. "I think I've learned there's no making up for what didn't happen in our lives," and then he added, "and time rushes by. Though it slows up here." Then abruptly David asked, "How are you feeling?"

"Old. Not always, just sometimes. I look at Betty, and Betty looks at me. I think of her way back then, and she must think of me then, and I know we are well along. And then, of course, the damn infarct. But let me pontificate a moment more. Knowing that there was, that there *is*, no way to live it all—that there are a thousand facets of ourselves that will never see the light of day, let alone real fruition, kills off all those useless self-hating regrets and should-haves and should-have-nots. It makes this aging thing a hell of a lot easier." He went back to his tea. David got up and poked around the fireplace, but there were no live embers, and he returned and sat down. After several minutes David said, "Me, a dozen failed relationships. Her, a failed marriage."

"I didn't know she was married!" This said in obvious surprise, and then Alan quickly added, "But why would I?"

"Yes, she told me on the phone, for five or six years, I think, a James or Jim."

"How long have they been separated"—he seemed flustered—"divorced?"

"I think a few years. You're surprised. Thought she was too sick?"

"No! I don't know." Alan seemed a bit distracted, but then went on, "She was certainly beautiful. Most wonderful brown eyes." And then he felt this was inappropriate.

David smiled and said nothing.

Now Alan got up and fooled with the fireplace.

"Some pretty sick people get married—even stay married," David said, and then he went to see a patient.

*

It was a math class. She was good in math. Mrs. Luntin said, "Muriel, tell me the answer." Was the name Luntin or Loontin? Was it Loony? It was Loony! That was it—Mrs. Loony! But she couldn't answer.

Her face got hot and still hotter. Mrs. Loony insisted. "Muriel, I want the answer!" Her face was so red now it glowed. Mrs. Loony insisted, "Muriel, you know the answer! Give it to me! Now!" and she pointed her finger at her. But Muriel couldn't talk. Muriel could take over and be in charge, but she had no voice. Didn't Mrs. Loony know that? Everyone else knew. David knew. And she wasn't Muriel now. She was Lisa, who talked only in rhymes and could not answer anyone who didn't talk in rhymes. And she knew nothing of math.

And then from the back of the room she heard David say, "This time no rhyme." She turned, and he smiled at her, and she turned back and was about to say, "Mrs. Loony, I'm Lisa." But instead she woke up screaming, "Jesus, Jesus, dear God, don't let it happen to me again—not now—not ever." But she knew Muriel was gone after all, and Lisa did not have to rhyme to keep her away.

Later in the day walking on Main Street, she thought about the dream and told herself that some anxiety was inevitable when old memories are reawakened.

Then she thought about the name of the teacher. It was Luntin—not Loontin or Loony—and she felt better.

And she asked herself about Muriel and recalled a session with Dr. Berman, her analyst. Who was Muriel, after all?—only an aspect of herself. And she had a thought that was entirely new to her. Muriel was a mood, a mood she used to get into, nothing more, and now she felt joyful and eager to see him—David.

*

"You call Alan, 'Alan.' "

"To you, but not when I talk to him," Bob answered.

"You're the only one who calls me Dr. Green around here."

"I know. I just find it hard."

"Want to keep your distance?"

"I guess so," Bob sighed—with resignation.

David thought of his own distance-making machinery of the past, his ancient dread of being touched, physically touched. It no longer plagued him, but it wasn't completely dead either.

"Can I tell you what I feel?"

"Sure," David said, attempting to be casual.

"I'm afraid I'll hurt someone—I never have. But it scares me. If I get close enough, I'll want to do something."

"What?"

"To hurt them," and tentatively, "David—to hurt them—especially girls."

"What about girls?"

But Bob was silent now. David said, "Look, a thought, a feeling is not an action."

"Oh, I'd like to get close to them. I want to get so close to them. I want to squeeze them—crush them—hurt them. I want to tell them I'm here. I want to come through the other side of them." Bob said this as if he meant it, but with little affect.

"When did you realize all this?" David asked matter-of-factly.

"In a session with my last shrink."

"His ideas, then—or do you really feel this way?"

"He said it, but it's true," Bob said defensively and after a minute of silence went on, "I believe it. I feel it. I want to hear them yell out." This last statement said with no emotional commitment, David noted to himself. Then out of the blue Bob said, "You don't take notes, do you?"

"No," David answered evenly, waiting for some kind of offensive action. But it didn't come. Instead Bob said, "I guess you think it's all a sex thing—me and the girls and all."

"Do you?"

"I don't know."

"Maybe you're angry," David suggested.

"I'm lonely. I'm awful lonely. I never felt anything else." His eyes reddened, and he quickly asked, "Can I go now?"

"Sure," and despite a reawakened aversion, David reached out at the door and patted him on the shoulder and shivered for a split second after Bob had gone.

III

JEAN and Lisa drove to the train in silence.

Before Lisa mounted the train stairs, Jean hugged and kissed her. "Nothing ventured, nothing gained," she said, and then added, "But minimal expectations, minimal disappointments." Then she laughed and said that she was "very high on clichés today."

Lisa shivered. She didn't know whether it was from the bitter cold or the anxiety. But the train car was warm, and when she was finally settled in her seat and the train started to move, she felt better.

Jean shouted, "Remember—call me—if anything you need—to say—to hear or anything. Tom and I love you."

Lisa waved, but said nothing.

*

When she stepped off the train, Alan ran over to her at once, hugged her hard and kissed both her cheeks.

"I knew you at once. My God, you are a beautiful woman."

"Alan, you've hardly changed at all," Lisa said as she looked about for David.

Alan quickly reassured her. "It was my idea. I insisted I come and get you. Told him he had to stay and hold down the fort." Then almost under his breath—"Easier for both of you."

She thought the station wagon felt like an office. As soon as they left the station, they were on snow-covered roads with large drifts on either side. They were in the mountains, climbing higher, quite isolated, and she thought of the route to Shangri-la. Then she laughed inside at her picture of Alan as the high lama. The high lama taking her to David. None of the land was familiar to her, and white snow in every direction didn't help. And she realized with a start that she had seldom been off the grounds of the place when she had been a student there.

She said very softly, "I know he's afraid too."

"Too?" Alan asked.

"Yes. Strange, and yet after all these years not so unusual."

"How so?"

"Guess we're afraid of our own feelings—how we will react—all this time that's passed. Do you feel all right, Alan?"

"So-so. Yes—I'm fine. Dr. Berman told you about my coronary?"

"Yes. I meant to call. I was having terrible trouble with James—my former husband."

"What work does he do?"

"An artist, like me, and also an art director in an ad agency. But that's done now. It's been some time." After a minute or two of silence she went on, "Me and Jim—that was another life. I guess I've had several."

"Several?"

"Lives," she said.

After a few minutes of hesitation, Alan asked carefully, "How do you feel, Lisa?"

"Good! I feel good. I've been put to the test a number of times—and no collapse—no splitting—no Muriel," she said quietly. "How is David?" she added brightly.

"Fine, fine."

He drove slowly and with great caution. The snow was lightly coming down again. She recognized a few landmarks. We are almost in the valley of the blue moon, she said to herself.

"He's a good doctor," Alan said with some enthusiasm, "a good therapist, and he makes my life easier."

"Always was," she murmured.

*

It was six in the evening and pitch dark out when they arrived. But the lights on everywhere throughout the buildings in the clearing completed her illusion of a small mountain village. Lisa told herself that it was Shangri-la after all and surely was back then, too, but she was too sick to know it at the time.

And then she was in Betty and Alan's house being hugged and kissed by Betty, a large, affable, gray-haired woman of sixty. The house radiated light and warmth, and Betty told her that she'd "know her face in a second." Lisa said very little. She had had almost no contact with Betty in the old days.

Betty showed her to her room upstairs and gave her fresh soap and towels and said they would all have dinner in an hour or so.

99

In her mind's eye she saw herself stepping into a Grandma Moses painting she was particularly fond of and she thought, Time stands still here.

And he was there when she came down and so were Betty and Alan and an elderly, heavy woman who turned out to be the housekeeper.

She said, "Hello David," and he said, "Hello Lisa," and they both had concurrent attacks of severe shyness. No kissing, Alan noted—as did Lisa and David, and Betty. Actually, they shook hands rather formally.

Alan made several awkward attempts to start conversations. Mostly, they wound up as fractured dialogues between Betty and himself.

David said almost nothing.

Lisa tried to be interested; but it didn't work. Fortunately, she was so tired she didn't much notice her anxiety.

After dinner they lingered around the table, and on request Lisa described her work as a painter—"representational," "old-fashioned"—and said that she also did book jackets. Betty's further encouragement brought out Lisa's modest success in galleries in New York and Washington. Her fatigue became apparent, and Alan suggested that she might want to go to bed—and so the first several hours of an odd reunion ended.

*

He told himself he was in love with her. He felt dislocated and slept poorly.

She verbalized nothing. She knew how she felt. She slept soundly.

*

Bundled up warm against clouds and cold, they walked slowly, side by side, in a large wide, open field covered with snow.

"I knew in a very short time that private practice was not for me. Among other things," he gestured with his hands, "I couldn't stand the idea of selling my services."

"I've had a hard time letting go of paintings. God knows I've wanted them to sell and then had all kinds of sinking feelings when they were carted away—to belong to someone else. Still feel that way."

"No," he quickly responded, "it's not that I wanted to withhold or not give of myself. I think I can do that all right." He stopped. "What am I saying? Jesus! Maybe I can't do it at all. Maybe you're right."

"I'm right?" She seemed a bit annoyed. "What do you mean I'm right? I only said that parting with pictures is hard." And then she gently added, "I'm not suggesting you can't give of yourself."

David nodded his head. "But it's true—history—personal history bears it out. What I can give of myself is decidedly limited."

"Do you give less of yourself here than in private practice?"

"I don't know. Maybe. Less responsibility."

Without awareness they had wandered a considerable distance from the buildings. The snow was quite high near the edge between the clearing and the thick woods. Lisa made a snowball and then threw it straight down forcefully so that it made a vertical tunnel into the snow. She thought of James and felt irritated, realized that James never showed her any sign of vulnerability, and then felt better.

David went on, "Alan is in charge. I can always go to him. Sounds terrible, doesn't it?"

"Yes, if it's true." She added, "But you just don't strike me that way."

"Maybe the involvement. With Alan here—I don't feel that caught up—trapped."

Their faces were cold, but neither of them made a move back toward the houses. They walked now in small circles and had made a jumble of many footsteps in the snow.

"I hated to be in business. I hated to sell slots of time—and what felt like pieces of myself."

He made a snowball and threw it at a broad oak tree, missed. He shrugged his shoulders and smiled. This affected her, and she had no interest in why it did. She felt like hugging him to her, but said and did nothing.

"I felt like a goddamn salesman," he went on half-smiling sadly. "Sounds like clichéd analysis, but I felt like my father—he was in business—actually a salesman—and I knew he hated it—but he was trapped. Time just passed, and he couldn't get out."

They started to head slowly back in the direction of Betty's house.

"Jesus," he sounded genuinely disgusted, "all this self-serving crap. Tell me about you—why did you want to see me?" He caught himself and laughed, obviously embarrassed. "There I go with me—me again—forget it—ridiculous question in any case—just tell me about you."

"What do you want to know?" He loved her eyes and

her mouth and how she spoke and pulled her knitted wool hat over her ears periodically.

"Anything. Tell me anything that comes."

"You sound like an analyst now."

"I'm sorry."

"Well, I felt I owed you a lot." She hesitated. "What I felt—I never got you out of my mind—" Now she felt embarrassed.

"We owed each other a lot," he quickly added. "If you had not been here, I'd have never left or come back. Got to leave to come back," he laughed.

They walked with their heads down now, looking at the fresh snow they had not made footmarks in yet.

"I hated you. I loved you," she said softly.

They were adjacent to the library now.

"God," she suddenly burst out. "You never came back once to see me—not a letter—a phone call—a card. Your caring saved me." Her eyes were red now and full of tears. "It took me longer—to do it—to get out of here. I swore I'd never come back. Not to any hospital"—she spoke quickly—"and not to any so-called school either. But you got me out. *You*—your feeling for me—and then nothing—nothing. Was I fooled? Was I fooled?" Neither of them said anything for a minute, and then she cried out, "That's why I had to see you. For all these years the goddamn question has been poisoning me. Was it all nothing—just a game?"

He spoke very gently. "If it had been a game, I never would have gotten well enough to leave. Don't you remember how terrified I was of being touched—emotionally, physically? I couldn't stand feeling anything. When I said, 'A touch can kill,' I meant it. I was crazy and I'll tell you something I haven't told anyone in years—residuals are still there. And maybe that's why I'm still here. I think we never get over anything completely. But it was no game. How I felt about you and I knew you felt about me made me sane—and—" He was suddenly at a loss for words.

She was calm now. They were both calm. But David felt very sad.

"Then why didn't you come, call, something?" And then she added, "I'm making all kinds of claims. You owe me nothing." She laughed, "You see I've been in analysis, too."

"I cared," he said softly.

Their faces were very red now, and it was extremely cold, but they lingered outside for a few more minutes.

"You know. Residuals. You remember Muriel. I'm still afraid. I still dream."

"I cared," he said.

"And now?"

"More. Even more now."

She reached up and kissed his forehead and saw the tears in his eyes.

*

"Of course they were sick," Alan told Betty.

"She's the only one I ever met who spoke in rhymes."

"Ritualistic—a defense mechanism." He smiled. "Takes talent."

"Calypso singers do it," Betty offered.

"Never thought of that," he said. "In schizophrenia and other conditions there are sometimes clang formations—the sound association becomes more important than the meaning association. But this wasn't true of her. Everything she said was logical and decipherable but was said in rhymes."

"He spoke to her in rhymes?"

"She'd ignore anything else. All dialogue had to rhyme."

"What a strain."

"He started out feeling challenged, and got very good at it. The rest of us—her therapist, John—couldn't do it—not really."

"Defend against what?"

"What do you mean?"

"You said it was a defense."

"She was a dual personality—Lisa and Muriel. Muriel was grown up, assertive—even aggressive—angry, but mute. This made it safe. Her anger couldn't be expressed. Lisa was sweet and childish and afraid of Muriel and what she represented, growing up, anger, assertion. She eventually told David that talking in rhymes kept Muriel submerged. That was the defense—against those aspects of herself she couldn't accept. Eventually she did accept them and growing up—and a good deal of what we call integration took place."

"You certainly helped her."

"I did not! Neither did her therapists before she got here nor John—until David got involved. It was David. A therapeutic chemistry between them."

"You mean love."

"All right," he smiled, "love."

"Is she really well now?"

"I don't know. What's 'really well'? Of course she's still Muriel and Lisa and all those aspects of herself represented by those roles. We're all multiple moods, urges, impulses, needs. I guess to the extent that they're not repressed and split off into autonomous separate bundles, she's well."

They sat in silence a while.

"She seems more Muriel to me now than Lisa," Betty said.

"How so?" he asked.

"Mature, assertive."

"Interesting," he said. "She identifies herself as Lisa and accepts the healthy feelings and abilities of Muriel. But, you know, she loved to draw and paint even in those days, and it was mostly as Lisa."

"Finally has them together—integrated."

"The left and right sides of the brain."

"What?"

"Recent work. They believe one side is for intellectual work, the other for creative aspects."

"What about him?"

"What do you think?"

"He seems fine. Though he's alone so much. There's no woman in his life, at least lately. I think there is now."

"He was badly damaged when he got here. Chronically depressed and terrified of closeness, which he concretized into a phobia about being touched. Obsessed with time and time's passing. I can understand that part of it now—time passing—better than ever before. But he is brilliant—a superb mind—all blocked then by intense rage, which terrified him and was mainly expressed through sarcastic remarks. He was obnoxious and needed people—a hell of a combination. But she touched him."

They sat quietly for a while, both thinking, and then Alan went on. "It started out as an intellectual exercise for David. He was very well read—in psychology— psychiatry—was ahead of most of the teachers—gifted in math, physics. He wanted to understand her. Saw her as a case—an intricate watch—watches fascinated him. She was a challenge, and he had also developed a rivalry with John. But there was more there than he knew. No one ever told him about countertransference and big brown eyes."

"So she touched him," Betty laughed.

"Emotionally and eventually physically too."

"You mean—"

"No! Nothing like that. Just touching hands. For him it was a major step. In a way he was the sicker of the two. It was really more of a delusion than a phobia. He believed a physical touch could kill, and no attempt to link it rationally to his fear of emotional involvement could help a bit. As a matter of fact, he wouldn't listen—his resistance was enormous."

"But he somehow got her to touch him."

"In a way that was true. He saw her at least in part as his creation. Anyway she was his bridge to reality."

"But you surely played a role?"

"Yes. Of course I did. We certainly worked on his rage and his newfound feelings for her. I made use of everything I could. I suppose in a way I still am his therapist. I ought to let go. I ought to throw him the hell out of here. I tell myself if I never had the heart attack, I would, and let's wait and see how I feel—but—" and he shrugged.

"Of course you'd miss him."

"My star patient and protégé—*I* should talk about countertransference. But make no mistake. She touched him. Without her, nothing of great significance would have happened. And yes—of course, I'd miss him."

In bed that night Betty held his hand, kissed him, and wanted in some way to reassure him, but didn't quite know how.

*

They had drinks in his office.

"I feel that I'm back in another life—another time—another mood."

"Another dimension," he added.

"I feel I somehow did step back. It's—"

"Step back?" David seemed a bit alarmed.

"I don't mean regressed." Lisa laughed. "Just a mood I forgot about—one I haven't had in years." And then, laughing again, "You know, even at best, artists are kind of crazy. Sometimes they will do just about anything—look anywhere to find the right mood."

"I know writers often move about—home to home—to try to recapitulate moods and feelings they need in order to write."

"Sounds like the same thing. Have you been writing, David?"

"No. I'm afraid I'm not very creative. And not eager to give up a good mood when I find one."

They both felt very good—warmed by the drinks and the fire.

"Beethoven moved more than forty times."

"Anything for art."

"Do you feel that way, Lisa?"

"No. Not at all," she said emphatically and then added in a much softer tone, "I guess I believed, anything for love."

He felt uncomfortable and changed the subject. "Would you like to go out for lunch tomorrow, or dinner?"

"You mean leave the grounds?"

"Yes."

"I don't know if I want to change the mood."

"Into the other dimension," he said. And she added, "The real one."

But the snow was very heavy, and they couldn't leave.

"Reality strikes again," she said.

They were just about able to make their way from building to building.

Only a handful of students remained for the holiday, and they visited a few special classes that went on but didn't stay in any for long.

They spent most of their time in the library—a large beamed, paneled room with a huge fireplace—reading, talking, and reminiscing. She was reminded of a holiday she spent with Jim in Zermatt. He had become enraged at a supposed infraction she'd committed but could no longer remember. His vindictive tirade was one of many that occurred during their marriage. She told David about this and other aspects of her marriage and her work. He told her of several serious attempts at lasting relationships. These resulted in severe enough anxiety to necessitate a brief return to psychotherapy. He told her about his training, his work in hospitals, and his current job.

At one point on their way to the dining room David saw Bob Mathis. He wasn't sure Bob saw him and he somehow felt very self-conscious.

*

They sat in the diner drinking coffee. She seemed to be off somewhere—drifting. He watched her for a few minutes and then spoke.

"Is the moment over?"

"The moment?"

"The mood? Does this place spoil it?"

"No. Not at all. Just thinking about James. He hated to be called Jim—" and she hesitated.

"Go on."

"You sound like my analyst again."

"Are you still seeing him?"

"James?"

"No. Your analyst?"

"No. We stopped—almost two years ago."

They sat silently for a while.

"Why did it break up?" he asked.

"I ran toward him. He ran away from me," she said simply.

"Resignation," he said.

"Resignation?"

"Resignation and detachment. Inertia and distance. The substance of my analytic problems these many years."

"You think James and you are alike?"

"I don't know him. What do you think?"

"You're not at all similar. He had a cruel streak. He was pompous. Vindictive!"

"Detachment is excellent protection," he said.

1 1 0

"I can tell you that passivity is not. That's what we worked on for years—Dr. Berman—self-effacement and rage—Muriel—the angry one!"

"But you believe that's what happened to us too?"

"What?"

"You ran toward me, and I ran away from you?"

"That was a thousand years ago," she said.

*

"I saw you with that woman," Bob said.

"How come you didn't go home for the holiday?" David asked.

"It's lonelier there than here, and I'd only have to come back."

After several minutes of silence Bob said again, "I saw you with her."

David said nothing.

"You're lucky."

He still said nothing.

"You seemed happy with her."

He tried turning the session to other areas, but this only led to long silences.

He spoke about the fear of rejection and how freeing it could be if a person could learn to live at peace with rejection—if rejection was acceptable without self-hate. But Bob would not bite. Going out the door, he said, "She likes you. The way she held your arm and looked at you. I could tell."

*

"I want to go to bed with you."

"When?" he asked.

111

"Now!" she answered.

"Do you feel it's been years—do you feel awkward?" he asked.

"No. I feel we never stopped. And you?"

"As though we've been together all these years," he said.

They made love in his room. It was gentle, warm—a meld for both of them. Rather than the usual excitement he felt he was in a kind of haze—a golden haze. He thought of a meadow—a picture he once saw—and he felt very young again and fell asleep.

She felt motherly—soft, warm, and motherly. The sensation was a mélange of contentment, fullness, and wholeness—something she had never quite experienced before.

*

"It's a rare thing, isn't it?"

"What?"

"To get back the girl that got away."

"And the boy that got away."

"I'd like to stay here forever," she said, "but—"

"But what?"

"We are not teenagers anymore—and not sick or so sick, I hope."

"What are you saying?"

"This is not the real world."

"It's my world—my real world. It's Alan's world. It could be yours too. The summers here are incredible. Tanglewood—the music—artists flock here. Jacob's Pillow—dance festival."

"No. And it's not the real world for you either—" And then very gently she said, "It's your sanctuary, and Alan's sanctuary too."

"Lisa—we're doctors—I mean, this is our profession."

"I know. But it's still your sanctuary, and you know it." She quickly added, "I know how you feel about selling time—private practice—but this place—it's idyllic, David—but it means—staying a child."

"What about the mood—the other day?"

"I think painting needs what living needs."

"What does that mean?" he asked with poorly concealed irritation.

"It means more than a mood. It means connection—reality."

"I have to see a patient," he said abruptly.

"I hurt you."

"No. Yes. I don't know. I'll see you in a while." He stalked off, and she remembered similar partings years earlier. She thought about Jim and that perhaps he was right. He said she wanted a man for herself, all for herself, no sharing with anyone, anything, anyplace.

"What is so wonderful about the real world?" she asked herself but quickly put this thought aside and forgot it.

*

"Your anger?"

"I don't feel it now."

"You said you want to hurt them."

"I know. But what I feel right now is lonely."

"You feel I'm not with you—on your side?"

"I don't know. I just feel that I'm always lonely."

113

"Do you contribute to it?"

"You think I do?"

"How do you feel about it?"

"I just don't know."

They said nothing for several minutes.

"Now I feel angry."

"Yes," David encouraged.

"I feel—caught—trapped."

"Go on, Bob," David said encouragingly, "how?"

"I'm not sure—I guess what I feel is I want to hurt them again. But I don't know why."

"Do you really want to be with them—with someone—a girl—and at the same time want to pull away—afraid?"

"My trap?"

"Does it feel right?"

"Yes." He was more animated now. "But why do I want to pull away? Afraid of what?"

"Yes—of what?" David asked as he thought, The story of my life.

"Like I'll get lost." Bob frowned and became silent.

"What are you feeling?"

"I had a fantasy."

"What?"

"Drowning—me drowning."

"Getting close to them—to someone—is drowning?"

"That's how it feels."

*

"You could work in a hospital. You don't have to be in practice."

"Why is that better than working here?"

"You know why." She was annoyed.

"I don't know why." He was sullen.

"You needn't live on the grounds. Your life would broaden out—and—" she hesitated, "you'd get away from Alan."

"Jesus—I thought you liked Alan—and Betty."

"I love Alan. You know that doesn't have a damn thing to do with it."

"Are you jealous, Lisa?" His tone had changed. He was gentle now—no trace of being surly.

"Maybe I am. But it changes nothing about the value of you getting out of here."

Now he was irritated.

"Jesus Christ! It's almost as if you came here to get me out."

"It's possible. But I never had it in mind—consciously, that is."

"What did you have in mind?"

"To seize that rare opportunity, I guess. To see the boy, the one who got away—and maybe the mood, too—the mood—as you said, the moment—a feeling I thought was gone—over. Maybe you could call it love."

He was touched by her words but he moved them aside.

"Do you know what working in a state hospital is like?"

"No."

"It's a kind of Auschwitz. It would make me feel like a Nazi."

That night he had a dream—it was actually a close recapitulation of a night on duty when he worked in a state hospital.

He was there again, trapped. He had finished with the place—why was he there again?

He was the doctor on duty. In this dream, he was asleep in the doctors' night room. In the dream within that dream he woke to a scream—not his own. The radio music and the thin door separating the duty room from the ward could not shut out real noise. Then, when he woke in the current dream, he wasn't sure if he heard it or it was part of a dream. Maybe he had screamed after all. He dressed quickly. The attendant outside the door on the ward side held a man, actually supported him, who then screamed again—this time in David's face. In the dream he said to himself that he had not dreamed it—and it had not been his own scream, and he felt relieved.

"Sorry to get you up, Doc." This from the attendant, whose voice sounded odd. Then he saw the attendant's face. It was Lisa. David said, "I told you it is like this."

"Sorry to get you up, Doc," she said again, and he knew it was Muriel and only nodded.

The man dripped blood—David realized—from his upper chest—soaking his pajama top.

"Did it with a broken glass," the man said proudly and screamed again.

They propped the man up and half-carried, half-dragged him through the ward full of beds. Some of the patients jeered. Some laughed. Most paid no attention at all. One excited man peed against a bedpost.

The attendant, now a man, lunged at him, nearly dropping the bleeding man's head. "I'll get you later, you son of a bitch," the attendant snarled. The man continued to pee and giggled to himself.

Now David was cool. He was the doctor in charge. They had to get the bleeding man to the treatment room to sew him up. David was cool—so cool he felt nothing. He asked out loud, "What has this got to do with psychoanalysis?" "Doctor Shmockter," the attendant suddenly screamed at him, and he woke up. His first thought was a mind picture of Lisa, and he hated her, and then in his mind's eye he saw her eyes and felt very sad.

*

"She wants me to leave."

Alan said nothing.

"You don't seem surprised."

"I guess I'm not. How do you feel about it?"

"I think it's goddamn crazy. I haven't seen her in a —a thousand years, and she comes here and wants me to leave."

"You invited her."

"She sent the note."

"What do you want to do?"

"Stay, of course."

They were silent for several minutes, and then David said with irritation, "She acts as if I've been here forever. It's less than three years."

Alan said nothing.

"How do you feel about it?" David asked hesitantly.

"There's a good deal you can still learn here." Alan felt hesitant and awkward.

"Of course there is!"

"And frankly I guess I've taken it for granted that you would take over after me."

"Jesus, Alan—please don't do that 'after me' stuff."

117

"I've had a major heart attack. Avoiding issues doesn't change reality."

"You're doing great. You've given up cigars."

"Reality, David."

"What's so hot about reality? Besides, I've seen at least several self-fulfilling prophecies."

"Listen, David—my point of view is selfish or at least self-serving."

"So is mine—so is hers. The whole thing is crazy. I'm going nowhere—nowhere at all! I'm happy here."

"Will you be after she's gone?"

"You've always asked the damnedest questions."

Alan poured some tea. He asked David if he wanted any, and David shook his head no.

"Sure, there is a chemistry between us. So what? We're adults, for Christ's sake. My life is here. I like it." After a minute, "I need it."

"There's also history between you."

"History, chemistry." He pictured her face, her body, her voice.

"Chemistry, history—Betty would call it love."

"I don't care what it's called. Love is not everything. Jesus, just like two kids. Too much has happened. We're not the same people."

"Would she stay here?"

"No," he sighed. "Says this is not the real world. Loves being a kid. The mood here—loves it, but that Shangri-la can become hell—that it's really an insidious kind of poison."

"I see."

"She says she can only work—paint as an adult— live, really live, as an adult—in the real world." Then he suddenly became angry and disgusted. "It's all a crock. It's really all a crock."

"I don't think so. Sounds like her analysis worked."

"Are you telling me I ought to leave?"

"Listen, David. I'm more selfish than you think. Don't expect to get any push from me. Better yet, don't trust me in this. Because I want you to stay." He hesitated for half a minute, then went on in an uncharacteristic rush. "In my heart of hearts I wish to hell she never came back. And I'm ashamed and I wish I was young again. No heart attack—" and he ran out of words and stopped.

David got up impulsively, hugged him, and left.

*

They had a snowball fight and they laughed a great deal and had a very good time.

Later, while she was reading in the library and he was writing medication orders, he had an intrusive thought. How much of the exuberance of the snowball fight came from anger with each other? He remembered one point in the fight when they were pelting one another quite hard.

That night they made love and were particularly tender. She did not go back to her room in Betty's house that night.

*

"Some humility! You're his disciple, and he won't let you go."

"Not true! You're going too far with the Shangri-la metaphor."

Her tone changed. She became softer.

"He has Betty. Who do you have, David—really have?" They said nothing for a minute and then very gently she asked, "Who have you had, really had all these years?" Then still gentler, "Who will you have when I leave?"

"Can't we talk about anything else?"

"I'm sorry, I suppose so."

But they didn't talk. They just wandered about outside from place to place until it became too cold. Then she took his hand and led him back to his place.

Their lovemaking was more turbulent, and he momentarily thought of the snowball fight. But the golden haze was still there for him, and the feeling of fullness was there for her.

And then they did talk.

"Are you afraid of me?" she asked.

"Like Bob," he said.

"Bob?"

"My patient—the young boy I've been seeing in therapy."

"How is he doing?"

"Afraid of his feelings—and his feelings are strong."

"And yours, David?"

He sighed, "You paint pictures in my head, Lisa. Golden meadows—hazy, summer day, golden meadows —even as it snows outside."

"And you would give them up—the pictures—to stay here?"

"What do you give up if you leave me here?" he asked.

"Oneness, fullness, strength, aliveness from deep inside, and contentment that I never knew existed."

"And you would give that up?"

"I would," she said sadly but firmly.

"Why? Are you so sure it isn't some kind of pride thing you're caught in?"

"I'm sure!"

"Then why?"

"Because it wouldn't last. Not here! It couldn't. This is a hothouse for growing dreams. But dreams don't last—and I'd wilt and die in a hothouse. I need—we need people, places—everything out there in the real world."

"Bob says he's drowning."

"Here?"

"No. When he thinks of getting close to a girl. That she will swamp him—inundate him. He will drown in her, and there will be nothing left of him."

"You are afraid of me."

"Not of you. Maybe of feeling too much and too good and of the kinds of losses that inevitably follow."

"Perhaps James was right about me."

"How so?"

"That I clung. Gave him no breathing space."

"Maybe."

"Is that what you believe, David—that I would drown you?"

"I don't know. I know I can't leave. I know you can't stay."

Her mood abruptly changed. She was visibly hurt and angry.

"I can't. I won't! But if I did, I think it would pall on you—let alone me. I think you're stuck here."

She dressed hurriedly.

"Where are you going?"

"Nowhere just yet," she said and then added, "I think you're stuck here. I think Alan will never let you go." And then, after a minute of silence, a rush of words, a torrent she couldn't control, with a sharp, bitter, vindictive edge in her tone—"You're the little boy, the precocious little boy. Alan is the daddy. Betty is the mommy, and at the same time you can stay detached, aloof, and above it all. Keep your precious freedom, your distance. You don't ever have to grow up. You can be like James—like so many other little boys I've met out there—and none of them will ever grow up, and neither will you, Alan, or Betty." She was breathless, as much from the surprise of her vindictiveness as from the effort of her rendition.

He said nothing. She was fully dressed now.

After a few minutes she said, "I think I should leave this place now. Maybe we should get together after a while—outside—not here."

"No," he said gently, "don't leave."

"I think I must," she said just as gently and then plaintively, "Please leave with me."

"I can't."

"Then call me and come to see me."

"No, stay."

"I was a fool to start this."

"Don't reproach yourself. I suspect I'm the inflexible one."

"Then perhaps I'll come back."

*

Rowayton seemed crystal-clear, alive, and full of people, even though it was actually underpopulated in the winter. The beach and sight of the water felt particularly good, and the house—her house—was wonderful. But he was there in her mind all the time, and after three days, being home again just felt like being home always felt before she left—except for him in her head.

"Everything here is the same. But my life has changed. I'm changed."

Jean said nothing.

"I obsess about him all the time."

"How much of him is fantasy—like a painting—your own construct?"

"Not much."

"How do you know at this point?"

"I don't idealize him. I know his faults. Why this idiotic attachment to detached men? Do I see them as strong, responsible?"

But before Jean could answer, she answered herself. "He's anything but strong. I know that. If anything— he makes me feel strong. We go back a long way. I've thought about it a great deal. We are damaged people, David and me."

"Who isn't?"

"Not the same. Together we made a whole person. Maybe now we can be two whole separate people to- gether. He's the doctor. Why can't he see that?" She laughed and then was dead serious again. "But he can't, won't leave there. He said, 'We have history together, the most important kind of history,' but he stays there —and lets me go."

"You've idealized those times together—when you were kids and now too. We all have someone from the past who connects us to then and to being young too. I suspect being in love with *then* is not so unusual. And I suppose we confuse it with thinking we love the person who connects us to it."

"No! My so-called young life was a nightmare."

"When you helped each other, that changed, didn't it? Isn't that the so-called beautiful history you shared together?"

"Only for a short time and—then he left."

"And you extended that time. You fantasized about it all these years and about him."

"It's possible," she sighed. "I may be in love with a fantasy. But I'm in love with him too."

After a few minutes of silence—"He's nothing like James. He's gentle, understanding—really quite open."

After a few minutes she asked, "Do you think it would have been different if you had not gone back there—if you met elsewhere?"

"No. Staying there would still be the same issue for him. And it goes beyond the place. It's us. It's a question of commitment to us."

＊

"Do you remember how obsessed I was with time?" he asked Alan.

"Of course. The first time we met, you commented about my clock not going and wanted to know the make of my watch."

"You have a great memory."

"Curse of the trade."

"The main thing was that time went so fast. It all felt

so short to me—a lifetime and then it would be over for all time. Now, without her—time feels long and heavy and barely drags by. Her coming back," he shook his head, "why did she have to come back?"

"Reality intrudes."

"The past intrudes."

"It's always there, of course—in the so-called present."

"Attacks from unexpected quarters."

"Attacks?" Alan asked.

"Attacks of reality—and dislocations, and I suppose the establishment of new centers of gravity."

"Could call it adjustment or adaptation."

"Or growth," David added, and then with a half-smile, "But what if you're just not ready for it—to grow?"

"Conflict."

"Conflict and anxiety," David said and then added, "stultification."

"Or resignation."

"But I've been happy."

"Really?"

"Comfortable."

"I don't sell comfort short. These days I respect it much more than exhilaration."

"After a thousand years."

"A thousand years?"

"Something Lisa says. God, she got herself together—and following a divorce yet."

"Maybe the divorce followed getting herself together."

"Me, the analyst," he snickered at himself. "She came a lot further than me, I suspect."

"Running races?"

"Alan, she seemed so sick when we were kids. Was I that sick? It was bad. God knows it was bad, but was I that sick?"

"How sick is sick? Who isn't sick?" Then gently, "You know better than that—all that quantifying—nomenclature nonsense. It's all used to dehumanize ourselves. Why get into it?"

"Of course I agree."

They sat silently for a few minutes. David looked at the clock and laughed, "Your clock is always on time now—my own inner clock is way off. I've been getting up at four in the morning since she left."

"Symptom of depression, Doctor."

"I know. I wonder how she feels. Can't be too bad or she'd come. This morning, couldn't sleep, had a crazy paranoid thought."

"What?"

"The years she waited here for me and I never showed up. Is she getting revenge now?"

"Is your pride keeping you from calling her?"

"No! It isn't pride at all. I wish it was. I could cope with that—I think. No—what it is, Alan, is fear—fear and confusion too."

"Dreams coming true—the good dreams can be difficult, easier to deal with wishes in fantasy—can have it all at the same time. No price to pay."

David did not respond. He was lost in thought for a minute and then he went on, "Why call her? I don't want to leave here. Maybe I can't right now. Of course, her answer is that I don't want to grow up. Isn't that something? I mean, the way she's rattled me. When we were kids, I played the therapist, at least I thought so. Now that I've become a professional therapist, I've become the patient, and she's the doctor."

"What's so bad about that?"

"There's the pride surfacing after all, I suppose. All I need is a dose of humility, and it all straightens out."

"Humility, the great pride neutralizer. Unfortunately, some of us need heart attacks to become human with ourselves."

*

"Why don't I tell him to go to her—to leave? Encourage him to get the hell out—to take the chance—to let himself fall in love with life? Time does run out. I should never have let him come back. Bad for all of us."

Betty was patient and gentle.

"Probably because you know he needs to be here. And aren't you getting a bit caught in this romantic thing? Maybe they'd be bad for each other. Falling in love with life is great, but he can fall on his face, too."

"Frankly that sounds omnipotent, and self-serving as hell, and hasn't a thing to do with the simple truth of needing him. I've become the dependent one! And I know more than anyone, there's nothing as selfish as dependency, however you rationalize it."

"Are you so lonely with me? How about all the years he wasn't here?"

"No! And maybe yes—not with you—with myself. To use the old parlance, I suppose I have a case of unresolved countertransference, and even the best rationalizations won't alter the truth."

"I'd just call it the empty-nest syndrome." Then after

a minute she said, "There are all the other people here. They need you. I need you."

"They are not David. He was always special. Talented. He's come such a long way."

"Because he became the doctor? Doesn't seem he's come as far as Lisa."

"That's part of it, I'm sure. You see, I'm not that emancipated from my pride that I don't want to recapitulate myself through a kind of professional progeny. Takes a special kind of humility to accept ending with one's own end."

"Don't chastise yourself for that. I would guess it's a common enough failing—mostly belonging to men."

After a long silence he said half-jokingly, "You know, the worst kind of pride is pride in humility. Then you have neither pride nor humility—all illusion."

She said nothing and then she asked, "Is it true that many analysts unconsciously marry their patients—I mean, on a nonprofessional level—and then go on analyzing their mates all their lives?"

"Yes—but you can't really tell who is the patient and who is the therapist."

"Maybe we are all patients," she said.

"And hopefully therapists too," he answered.

*

They strolled along Main Street. It was a sunny day, though still quite cold. A few people were puttering around their boats, anticipating the spring that was still a few months away.

"Why are you so insistent he leave the school? I mean, really why?" Jean asked.

128

"I told you. It's destructive. It wouldn't work. It's beautiful there, but it's—stultifying."

"How about bad memories? He was the brilliant one—disturbed—but not that bad—like you said—he even became the doctor—you were the real nut."

"No! Not true! When I went back—the place had no great significance for me—no bad memories at all. You have to understand—" She groped for the right words. They were standing still now at a space between the buildings where the boats were visible. "I'm not the same person. I was crazy then. It's as if I remember a person—not me—who experienced all that then—who just happens to be me now."

"Then what is it? Why does he have to leave?"

They started to walk again.

"He's got to leave—because I'm convinced he never did. He's the one—he must give up all of it—the whole scene—Alan included—or he will never be a whole person. I need a whole person."

"So it's a test?" Jean asked softly now. "And you are willing to take the risk of pushing this hard?"

"Perhaps it is a test, and perhaps it is time that I pushed hard for something I feel strongly about."

"Yes, but maybe it isn't a test of his willingness to grow up at all. Maybe your test has another rather ulterior motive."

"What?"

They stopped walking again.

"This could be nothing more than a test to see if he loves you enough to give it all up for you. If he passes —then he loves you more than his work, Alan, his current nice life. You become Miss Big in his life, and then you are reassured he will give you his all and not go the way of James."

Lisa was visibly shaken.

Jean said, "Though God knows James was a bastard, and I know very well the split had little to do with anything you did."

After a few minutes Lisa said, "It would feel easier if he at least called. I did make the first move." She hastened to add, "But I'm not angry."

"Why not?" Jean asked and then said evenly, "I see no halo around your head."

"Because I know he can't. I understand him—his problem. A call at this point would mean too much commitment—in the direction of here and of me—away from there. He's probably struggling to patch it up—to reestablish the mood of it all there, before I came along to upset it."

"Well—are you going to join him again or let him reestablish the old status quo? It could solidify—like cement—and put him out of reach."

"You think so?"

"I think so. But maybe I'm making more of my own feelings and opinions than they deserve."

They started to walk home.

*

"Do you think I will ever leave here?"

David pictured an old-age home and two wheelchairs—Bob in one, himself in the other.

"You will have to get out," David found himself saying.

Bob looked puzzled.

David quickly added, "Of course you will leave here.

This isn't your permanent home." He hesitated and then said, "You're not on the staff," and he felt this, too, was inappropriate and asked, "How have you been feeling?"

"Less angry."

"And your loneliness?"

"Not thinking about it as much, and I've been reading less. Talking to some of the other kids more."

"Good," David said, and he felt empty and depressed.

IV

WHEN Lisa called David, Alan and Betty immediately supported another visit.

This time David picked her up.

He kissed her forehead and gave her a single rose he had bought on the way. "Did you come to try again?"

"No, I came to see you."

"Then you've given up on me?"

"I can see this is it for you."

"But not for you?"

"Absolutely—not for me," she said with conviction.

The snow was fairly deep. It had not stopped since the morning. The plow had come through every four hours but could not keep up with the steady fall.

He drove very slowly.

They were both lost in thought.

She wondered why she had come. What could come of it? Life with Jean and Tom had been good. Uncomplicated.

He wondered if they would sleep together that night.

"Have you been painting?" he asked.

"I've tried, but it hasn't worked for me since I left you. No self-discipline, I guess—or not enough. How's your work been going—Bob?"

"Bob is concerned about leaving." He went on knowing he shouldn't. "He's afraid he will be stuck here forever."

"I don't blame him. Thank God I was no one's pro-tégé. Beware status protégé."

Why did I start this, he asked himself, and yet he went on. "He's not my protégé," he said wearily.

Lisa had energy. "Are you sure?" she asked and continued, "You were nobody's protégé when you first came here either."

He didn't answer.

She, too, did not like the wavelength they were now on, but she was energized and somehow felt forced to continue.

"What would you have been if you had never come here? Did you ever think of anything else?"

"I would have been crazy," he said simply.

"Are you so sure? What if you had treatment out-side?"

He laughed, "I had treatment outside. God! I never stopped being treated. I started seeing all kinds of therapists as soon as I started to talk in full sentences. By the time I came here, I was pathetic."

"You looked fine."

"Because I dressed neatly—obsessively neatly—everything in place. And I talked logically—so obsessively logically—everything in place. Do you know why?"

"Why?" she responded dutifully.

"Because I was in a chronic state of terror. If I let anything come out of place, I felt I'd come completely apart. Had I not met you and Alan, I'd be nothing to-day."

As they entered the school property, he voiced a thought. She couldn't tell if he was joking or serious or both. "I may have become an obsessive watchmaker. I was obsessed with time and every kind of timekeeping mechanism. That's what I always liked about the country, especially the mountains. Feeds the illusion that time slows down. It sometimes even seems to stand still, as if it isn't chopping you down relentlessly."

She gently answered, "And maybe it gives the illusion of remaining a child—always—even as you become very old—a very old child."

They were parked. Neither of them seemed to want to leave the car. But without the heater on, it started to get very cold. He suggested they go in. As they got out, she said, "I pictured us driving off and never coming back."

They slept together that first night back. But neither of them was responsive, and after hugging a while she went back and stayed the night at Betty and Alan's house.

*

Two days passed.

Lisa had spent some time with David, some with Betty, and much alone.

She visited several classrooms in session. But it seemed to disrupt the students, and so she stopped. Little had changed since her adolescence. She remembered her compulsion to paint on the walls and the long hours spent with John, her therapist. Neither nostalgia nor anxiety were stirred up. The scene was totally familiar but utterly lacked emotional investment. As she had told Jean, it was as if—now—she was viewing another person —a child—herself and yet not herself, in the setting then. A thousand years ago, she told herself.

She explored Lenox and found it to be charming and wondered if David could practice in a town that size—if it could serve as a transitional place or compromise.

Then she drove the school station wagon to Stockbridge and had coffee and wonderful apple pie at the Red Lion Inn. A man at least ten years younger than herself made conversation with her. She was amused but not particularly flattered. This had happened a number of times before. Stockbridge was beautiful. She could paint there, she told herself. But for how long? And then the whole idea of the Berkshire towns as compromise solutions palled on her. It was all too close to the school—to Alan. The break would not be a break unless it was complete.

And she had an insight. David had been in mothballs all these years. His training and living "outside" had been *protected experiences*, however horrendous some of it may have been. Had he really been out at all? She had been out. Her painting did not encapsulate her. He really is a little boy, she thought. But aren't all men little boys in large part? James had been a vicious little boy. The school, the storybook towns—these were not for her. She felt deeply about this and had the odd thought that Muriel would have understood.

When she got to Great Barrington—a gray, shoddy farm town—she felt her spirits lift. This was the real world—no storybook feel here—and by virtue of its being not uplifting it was uplifting. She saw some farmers and people who dressed and looked like factory workers and thought she could paint here. But the idea had no real appeal to her—too close to the school.

Strange—she barely remembered the towns as a girl. Did they ever leave the school? She thought they did, but she had been in a semianesthetized state all those years—in a fog, she thought.

Perhaps David had not extricated himself—yet—from that fog. Was he still back there?

As she drove the station wagon back onto the school grounds, she said out loud, "But I love him. He's the one. He's the only one I ever loved."

*

"She says I'm evolved but not evolved. She has a theory. Doctors, particularly analysts, never get the chance to grow up."

"Perpetual students?" Alan asked.

"More than that. She says they depend on patients to feel adequate about themselves and become as dependent on patients as patients are on them. They sit in their offices and stay out of involvement—the give-and-take of the real world."

"We've known all this for a long time. Sounds as if she's been giving it a hell of a lot of thought."

"She believes we live vicariously through patients and lose touch with reality—with the practical, detailed issues of living."

"Somewhat exaggerated—but a good sales pitch to get you into her 'real world.' Had no idea that she—she—" He seemed at a loss for words.

"That she could give an issue so much thought."

"You think I'm prejudiced against her—her intellectual ability, development?"

"Are you?"

My God, we've become adversaries, Alan thought. My God, Lisa and I have become adversaries. And then he said, "You may be right. Frankly, I'm tired of criticism of medicine and psychiatry, and doctors, particularly analysts, and the exaggeration of half-truths used in the service of personal hostilities and goals." He sighed. "But you may still be right. I still see her as she was then instead of now." He laughed self-derisively. "No wonder they don't believe in us. Me the therapist—I don't give ample credit to her years of treatment—and her experience and living all these years."

David said nothing. After a while Alan added, "More and more she sounds like a lot of person—a hell of a woman." But this didn't dissolve a feeling of tension that had just been generated between them. Then David asked, "How do you feel, Alan?"

"Old, David. Old and tired—for the moment anyway. David—you must listen to yourself—not to me, not to anyone." Alan smiled now. He felt a bit easier. "Just had the memory of my father, before he died, asking me, 'How did it happen—when—how did you become the father and me the son?' "

David smiled. "Do you think you've become the patient and me the analyst?"

"No. I think maybe you became the father, me the son, and Lisa the analyst's analyst."

"Or maybe we're the sons and she's the mother," David laughed.

*

It was early in the morning. They held hands in bed.

They could see out the window. It was sunny and bright, no snow falling.

"I feel like painting."

"Wonderful," he said. "We can buy your materials in town."

She pulled her hand away. Tears filled her eyes.

"What's the matter?"

"If you leave here, will you hate me?"

"You said you feel like painting. Why are you changing the subject?"

She was weeping now.

"I'm not changing the subject. You are becoming my muse. I feel like painting. I feel everything more when I'm with you. I'm getting more and more dependent on you."

"Is that so bad?" he asked.

"If I work here, I feel I will never leave. I'd be capitulating to something very sick in me—and in you. I just can't do that, or before long the painting would go bad. And—then—" She started to sob.

He held her close, stroked her head, and kissed her cheeks and eyelids and forehead.

"And if we leave—you will hate me—so will Alan. I'm trapped. I've gotten myself into a terrible bind."

"I'd never hate you. For a few seconds maybe, but not real hate, and Alan would never hate you."

"You would, you would," she sobbed, "you don't know it now, but you would."

"This time you're wrong, Lisa. I get angry—but hate is something else. Jesus, give me credit for something. Stop crying and listen. Christ! Listen to me!"

She calmed down, and he spoke quietly. "If I leave here, it will not be your decision. It's my conflict, you know, and it would be my decision—mine alone."

"Yours alone—due to my blackmail—my manipulations," she said bitterly and went on. "My tears, my misery—all of it real, but all of it mine. If I stay, I'll do the hating. If we go, you—"

He interrupted her. "You're dead wrong about it! I'm not as stultified as you think. Jesus—give me a little credit for growth. I'm not manipulated that easily. It pains me to see you cry. I can't stand to have you leave. But I have a hell of a capacity for being alone. If I leave, it won't be because of you. Stop being so damn omnipotent—so grandiose. Sure it would be because I want to be with you. But it would be my decision—mine only and my responsibility."

She started to weep again, softly.

"Maybe your conflict has less to do with here and more to do with commitment to me—to us," she said in almost a whisper.

"It's both, I'm sure. Involvement, commitment have not been my strong points. I've learned a little in treatment too." He smiled. "But the decision would still be my own!"

She cried, "Then you would hate yourself."

"Wrong again," he said and jumped out of bed and got her more tissues.

"That's something I don't allow anymore. I think I got at least that much out of treatment. I don't let it get past the first five seconds—*no self-hate*! So you better stop too!" But as he said this, he thought, By God, I'm actually talking about leaving.

142

She blew her nose. He jumped into bed, and they kissed—a long kiss—and they made love, quite passionately.

*

"I think you ought to leave."

"Why?"

"Because she's right."

"And you—for you—how do you feel about it?"

"Awful!"

"Then how can I leave?"

"I'll be all right." Time to tap my resources—what resources? he thought, and went on, "More important —how do you feel?"

"Mixed—very mixed—exhilarated at the idea— leaving and commitment, real commitment to her and very shaky about it, too, and—" he hesitated and then went on, "and guilty about you." Then after a pause, "Would we see each other?"

"I certainly hope so. Look—I have Betty."

"Yes, Lisa said that."

Then after a few minutes David said, "If I really go—I mean this whole thing, is it a surprise to you?"

"Deep down I knew it the first time, when I saw her get off the train. I knew she came to get you."

"Am I risking a great deal?"

"Yes. Anytime we get passionate about life, we risk a great deal. Fall in love with living or with anything or anybody and, more than risk, there's a guarantee of loss. We all die. But live it safe—no love—no loss—no surrender to anything, and there's no pain, but it's a walking death."

143

"What about Bob Mathis?"

"Bob will be fine! You're not omnipotent! We have other therapists."

Alan sipped his tea.

"She's really something—Lisa. Speaks well for treatment."

"Life itself can be a great cure," Alan replied.

David sighed. "I still have great doubts, not about her—or me and her—about me. I know I can teach, but private practice, even part-time?"

"You will be just fine."

"I love her and I'm in love with her."

"I know."

"The whole thing is amazing."

"That you got a second chance is rare."

"The girl and boy who got away."

"What is that?" Alan asked.

"Not important," David lied. And then on impulse he got up and hugged Alan and then quickly walked out. He did not see Alan's eyes fill with tears, because tears ran down his cheeks as well.

*

"Will we ever go back?" he asked. "I mean, to stay?"

The train made much noise on the track, so that she barely heard him, and she was drifting in a very peaceful half-sleep.

"I don't know," she said.

"Maybe if we are gone long enough," he almost shouted.

"When we are Betty and Alan's age," she answered sleepily.

"He said he'd be all right without me."

She could hardly hear him.

"Who?"

"Alan," he shouted.

"Yes," she answered, and after several minutes she fell into a deep sleep.

He couldn't sleep. He stared out the window at passing woods, fields, houses, and small train stations.

Then he was suddenly flooded with an enormous awareness of himself. No one else existed. He was becoming very anxious. He tried to turn it off, to think it away, but couldn't. He pictured running through the train in panic, screaming. He remembered a dream of running—many people about—he was naked. Now he was even less in control. He had a fleeting thought to wake her. But in his rapidly developing panic she did not exist. *He* filled his entire world. He was isolated.

I am having an anxiety attack, he said to himself— a panic reaction. It's been years, his own voice told him silently. And it went on—taking hold—spreading. He told himself that he could go back to the school—away from her. This didn't help. His heart was beating wildly now. His breathing was rapid and shallow. He couldn't get enough air. Hyperventilating, he told himself inanely. He was in a sweat. He felt the walls of the train closing in. He was going to lose touch—not know who he was. A depersonalized reaction, a voice in his head said. He was terrified. "I will go back!" he said out loud. "I will go back!" And now he felt he would explode— come completely apart into countless fragments.

Then it dawned on him that he was enraged—with her—and the attack lost its hold. It subsided. He felt chilled. He was exhausted. He was no longer alone. He was aware of other people on the train now. He looked at her. She slept peacefully. No one noticed him. He looked at his watch. Only a few minutes had elapsed.

"Ambivalence," he said in a whisper and thought of Alan saying, "Ambivalence—the human condition," and then a last jumble of questions about the future entered his mind, and as he said, "I love you, Lisa," he, too, fell asleep.